A Bad and Stupid Girl

A Novel

A Bad and Stupid Girl

Jean McGarry

The University of Michigan Press   *Ann Arbor*

Copyright © 2006 by Jean McGarry
All rights reserved
Published in the United States of America by
The University of Michigan Press
Manufactured in the United States of America
♾ Printed on acid-free paper

2009   2008   2007   2006   4   3   2   1

A CIP catalog record for this book is available from the British Library.

Library of Congress Cataloging-in-Publication Data

McGarry, Jean.
    A bad and stupid girl / by Jean McGarry.
        p.   cm.
    ISBN-13: 978-0-472-11580-8 (acid-free paper)
    ISBN-10: 0-472-11580-4 (acid-free paper)
    1. College freshmen—Fiction.   2. Roommates—Fiction.
3. Catholic schools—Fiction.   I. Title.
PS3563.C3636B33   2006
813'.54—dc22   2006010057

For Gina

PART ONE

Prelude

Siri was going to college, which would ruin her for life and then some. Her trunk was packed and its brass nameplate said: Sorenson, 4000 Mt. Hebron, Pleasaunce, New Federal. Her mother had packed each item in tissue. Layers of all one thing were bound in grosgrain ribbon.

Siri's mother's name was Sybele. There was a younger brother, Teddy, and of course, Dad, who'd retired from the Navy and was a decoy artist and investor. The house was white with six bedrooms and an attic paneled in cedar. The house had been built for the Sorensons and was settling nicely into the iron-rich clay of New Federal.

Teddy had his ear flush on that dirt while his mother packed his sister's trunk. He was pretending to be dead in battle, shot in the back, rolling in agony on his side. When he opened his eyes, his lashes whipped a spray of dew from the cold morning grass. He closed them and the cool beads felt like tears.

When his father left them every morning for the drive into Federal, Teddy was shot, bayonetted, trampled, or blasted and burned by man's evil force. Unless he had to go to school, in which case, his lunch was packed and tucked in a waterproof case like a pencilbox or a lady's purse. His father didn't carry a lunch, and neither did his sister Siri,

3

when she was a high school girl, just last year, one summer back. Teddy rode the schoolbus and often felt that shot, or blade or blast right there, but no time to croak in agony before the bus bucked and jerked and began to stink with the contents of the fourth and fifth graders parading on. Teddy was a first grader and small for his age.

Siri was small for her age, but Teddy had lost track of what her age was. Eighteen or nineteen or twenty. She was grown-up and a new book—that's what Dad had said, his glass tinkling with ice—was opening. For Teddy, it was closing, or—flaring his eyelids to fresh drops—it would close shut, now that his fine girl, perfumed and forever primping, was leaving home.

Leaving home was what he could not bear. How far? Too far for a walk but near enough to call on Sunday, which is what he heard them planning to do. Sunday was roast beef and a whole day of decoy ducks with the smell of turps and oil paint. Dad worked in his shed and sometimes on the breezeway. He had a studio over the garage with a bare lightbulb and books of models. Teddy went up there fifty times a day, up and down those steps, quiet as a mouse or cat with nine lives.

Everyone in the Sorenson family, including the cats with nine lives, had a part the house to themselves and Teddy did, too (the cellar, the backyard, mudroom, lavette and laundry room, Siri's closet and the shed where Dad's lumber and tools were kept and his paint cans and paint sticks), although Teddy, or Teddy-boy, as they called him, T-boy, roamed free, the only son. The attic was where they often found him, but he never stepped on a rusty nail or cut his eyes on splinters or caught his hair in live wires. Careful, be careful, boy—sometimes they called him boy or son. Baby-boy, never.

Siri Susan Sorenson, SSS, or 3S, was his sister's full name. Her boyfriend's name was Christo; he was the TV repairman's son and had no mother. They had known Christo "since year one," as his father liked to say, to show people (the next-door farmer, the housekeeper or the aunts who came for Christmas) how good a girl his sister was, and how close to home she kept. Going to college, yes, but Christo wasn't. He was doing what he always did—clerk at the fish and tackle shop on Hedge Cove, where he sometimes sold Dad's ducks, a canvasback or mallard.

Christo spent every day of the summer, after work and through the evening, with the Sorensons. He even helped with the packing.

But he wasn't there yet. It was just the two of them, mother and daughter, and T-boy outside the window, rolling on the grass.

The yard was wide-open space, a kingdom, as Siri saw it through the bedroom window. She was dressed in a slip and loafers. Her hair was dripping and this was the third time her mother had handed her the heavy pink hatbox containing the dryer with its plastic cap and coil of hose. If it dried like that, she'd have to cover it with a scarf. The curlers were spread on the dressing table. Her mother would roll the hair if Siri would dry it, then attend to her nails. The implements and polishes were laid out near a box of tissues.

Then, the tomcat wrastled a slipper underneath the bed and Siri turned to her mother: "You do it," she said.

And before long, the brother was in the room, scrambling under the bed and hauling out the big cat, hoisting it up on the bed to the tune of "Get him off!"

Teddy had an idea for a going-away present, "something to remember me by," as his mother liked to say when they were shopping at Christmas or for birthdays. At first he thought a dog—boxer or cocker spaniel like Aunt Bay and Uncle Dukie had, and got a new one when the old one died. Then another idea came to him out of the blue: a diamond ring like the one his mother had lost at the beach, left in the dressing room of the pavilion or slipped through the slats of the boardwalk, or just in the sand next to her beachchair made of a striped awning, which smelled of the attic. You could get a rubber ring in the gumball machine nested in a hard egg, but not every time, so he took himself a week before she left to the watchshop. His father was getting a haircut and had dropped him off at Christo's dad's TV and Radio. There were always some old men in there buying tubes or spark plugs, or just weighing them in their hands. Teddy left by the front door, the one that rang a jingle bell. Two of the TVs were tuned to the same boxing match, so no one noticed, or even if they did, so what? It was a free country, as he'd heard the fourth graders scream to the bus-driver when he told them to crank up the windows.

There was no one in the watchshop, waiting behind the counter. The man, an Italian with an extra eye strapped to his forehead and a garlicky breath, was in back to work under the hot lamps. Teddy let himself in quiet like a mouse or nine-life cat and found the ring he wanted—a blue cloudy stone with diamonds on each side. Price was seventy-two smackeroos, but he had a fifty-dollar bill, a twenty and a ten and a five from the time his mother emptied his bank and cashed the checks the Jesuit uncle sent every Christmas. Into the bank his mother had gone with the coins and checks and silver dollars and out came the brand-new fifty and twenty and ten that Teddy lay on the hot glass of the counter. He cooled his heels.

The Italian man with the three eyes was surprised, and said only one thing: turn out your pockets, kiddo, but then he spotted the fifty and twenty and ten and "What can I do for you, son?" he said in a nicer voice. "Who gave you this money? Does your mother know you're here? What's your name, Sonny?"

But nothing doing, no dice. No kid was coming in to his bonded store, as he told Teddy's father not ten minutes later, when his father caught up with him and Christo's father right behind him: it was not that kind of business. "Apologize to the man," his father said, but later he said that the watchman was just a "two-bit pawnbroker in merchandise of dubious origin and bona fides." But Teddy was in the doghouse too. Who had given him permission to take that money out of his dresser and onto the street? Shame on you, his mother said.

Tears and temper followed. And where was he left? On the outside looking in with nothing but nothing to give his sister, but he still planned to say goodbye and good riddance, because when they told her what he'd done, "announced it," she laughed her head off. "Fool," she called him. She called him nitwit and weirdo.

The hair was dried, brushed and rolled. Her nails were shaped and painted a milky pink. The car was packed and a family dinner, "the last supper," her father called it, took place at the Green Inn, with Christo and Siri's best friend, Irene, who was starting beauty school, but for now working at the telephone company. Siri received going-away presents from everyone (Teddy had wrapped up a twenty-dollar bill, "pin money," his mother called it), and her hair gleamed under the restaurant coachlamps. Real life was beginning and its first day was tomorrow.

Irene was dressed in her workclothes, a straight skirt and sweater. Her lap was wrinkled from sitting all day on a switchboard operator's high stool. She looked older than Siri, who looked older than Christo, who was very nearly a twin to Teddy.

Mother was smoking too many Chesterfields and Dad left his lighter out on the table so she could light her own. Irene smoked, too, when a cigarette was offered.

Siri Sorenson had never felt so smooth and finished. Even her innermost layer of clothing was new, washed and ironed with all the tags removed. She was too slim for her first panty girdle, but wore it anyway under a clingy jersey dress. Her face felt stiff, the skin heavy under a cementlike layer of liquid foundation with a dusting of silky powder. Her eyelids were sticky, as were her lashes, and her eyes stung. She felt as she had on prom night, girdled and creamed and packed and shaved, a tight and hard-to-open package. That night Christo was packed in his own scratchy rental suit. He'd never learned to dance and Siri protected her pastel pumps as best she could when the young couple took to the dance floor. Irene had a steady, who worked at Arthur Murray, and they danced like a dream.

Rick DelGiudice, the steady, was exactly the type Siri would have stolen from her friend if she wasn't so soon to leave for college. Over the summer Rick and Irene had double-dated with Christo and Siri, heavy dates with hours of parking in Rick's rebuilt T-Bird.

Sitting in back with Christo, watching what was happening in front, put Siri in a mood and she and Christo fought all summer, and the friendship ring of silver with a black pearl traveled back and forth. Christo now carried the ringbox in his shirt pocket. Siri did not want to discuss the "facts of life" with her mother, for she was sure her mother's understanding of these facts was superficial at best. But Sybele wished to speak to her grown-up daughter: it wasn't necessary with a local boy like Christo, a good Methodist or whatever he was, but college a hundred miles away was different and Mrs. Sorenson had bought a book early in the summer to prepare herself for this exchange.

It was Teddy-boy who got the lessons, or who valued them most. The mother-daughter talks took place late Saturday mornings in August after Sybele had shampooed Siri's hair and was combing it out. Siri sat at the vanity table looking at her mother's image in the mirror. That first time, Teddy was, by accident, hidden under the bed, where he had built a railroad switching yard for a matchbook train. He heard them splashing in his sister's bathroom, but shinnying out from where he was forbidden to go under pain of insult or slaps was risking it, so under he stayed and felt the whips of scented air flushed from the open door. "Don't rub so hard!" his sister said in that teenage voice which his father called "the martyr."

Fact one: mouthwash and underarm deodorant (sanitary pads he'd already seen and unwrapped).

Two: lower your voice and walk with a book on your head and your ankles crossed.

Three: clean, clean cotton

Four, Five and Six: Never let a stranger or strange boy "into"; tidy pocketbook; always flush; your "friend"; the fifth and sixth commandments (he looked them up, but they were no different from what he remembered).

By the end, Siri was blocking her ears, blowing her stack. "Stop it!" she said. "Leave me alone." That was when he popped his head out. By then, his mother was gone. "And you!" she said, seeing his face. "Get out of there and don't come back!" He got the blow on his back—hairbrush or curling iron—and went to find his mother. She was having a nap with a cloth over her eyes. She heard him coming and patted the spot next to her.

His father was supposed to "speak to" his sister, but everyone knew his father had nothing much to say to a girl Siri's age. Siri kept her door locked, just in case. Teddy knew because he had tried it. "It's you I'm keeping out," she said to his face, but T-Boy knew one good reason could hide another.

"Come to me, my melancholy baby," Teddy sang with his mouth at the crack of the door. He had heard his dad singing it as he painted the wooden wings of sitting ducks. Siri pretended not to hear.

I.

Her roommate Esther was reading in bed while Siri unpacked her trunk. The girls were introduced by the housemother, Mrs. Preston. Each had a bed, a dresser with attached mirror, a desk and a bookcase. The linen service was optional. Esther's mother had supplied matching plaid bedspreads and a rag rug. She expected Siri's mother to offer to pay for the extra bedspread, but Sybele thought her daughter should choose her own bed covering and planned to supply one in white chenille once she had the dimensions. When the Sorensons arrived at St. Mary's, Esther's mother had already made both beds and dolled up the room with the new rug and cotton-lace runners.

Siri knew her roommate's mother had been insulted by Sybele. (Siri had been calling her mother "Sybele" for over a year, but now she'd work it into conversations.) After the introductions, Sybele paced out the room, opened the window, then started to strip her daughter's bed of the hideous spread. Esther said nothing, but Siri told her mother not to touch anything, to leave it alone! Mr. Sorenson arrived in the nick of time. When he saw his wife with the bedspread bunched in her hands and that look on her face, he acted. He suggested that they go directly to the freshman reception, "out of harm's way," as he put it later.

Dad was fresh from the bursar's office, settling the fall-semester account. Esther was an in-state student and was boarding at St. Mary's on a math stipend. The Ferrys had no money—Siri knew this from the summer letters, but two seconds in the freshly painted room—Siri shut the window before even shaking hands—confirmed it, and it wasn't just the cheap, mill-outlet spreads with their metallic sheen; it wasn't just the mothball smell of ancient woolens; it wasn't the permanent waves that had conked Esther's and her mother's mousy heads; it wasn't even just the fact that mother, father and daughter had removed their shoes and were standing on the rag rug in their stocking feet. It wasn't any of it, but all of it. Siri already had them zeroed out, but that only made it harder for Sybele whose "faces" and "eyes," expressively aimed at her daughter, were ignored. Thankfully, Sybele, an alumna of St. Mary's, was eager to see what familiar face, with a daughter in tow, would turn up at the freshman reception. She was willing to be hauled off. Dad hadn't yet met the Ferrys, and he shook hands with the father, but the roommates needed get-acquainted time before the mothers posed too much of an obstacle.

Esther was reading *Time,* but she could still see the things—mostly underwear—the blond roommate was unwrapping from their tissue folds. Was she going to keep the trunk in their room? was what she said to this strange person. Siri said she didn't know. It could be used as a table, said Esther, if they decided to flout the rules about having a hotplate and provisions. With that, the magazine fell on her chest and she folded her hands on it.

Siri Sorenson had already told the roommate, Esther

Ferry, that she needed a lot of sleep and liked a dark room at night. Esther Ferry wrote back that she would do most of her studying in the library. She was an early riser and never missed breakfast. She planned to try out for freshman field hockey to avoid gym class. Siri didn't plan to do either. She had a letter from her doctor making the most of a slight heart murmur. She could not study more than an hour at a time and no all-nighters or football weekends, two-in-a-row. Esther was going to be a college professor and mathematician. The roommate from New Federal wrote back that she hadn't even chosen a major. College was her parents' idea, but she was looking forward to getting away from home.

Esther and Siri walked to the student union together, but separated at the door. Siri's mother had met friends and plans were being made for dinner in Boston with the daughters. Esther's parents were holding their plates of cafeteria food. They had saved a chair between them for their daughter, and now the college president would give her address. No, the nun said, don't stand. Stay where you are or come up and get some supper and punch. She would only take ten minutes of their time to welcome them to SMC and give them a bird's-eye view of the academic year and the programs planned for parents to keep them in touch with their freshmen girls, away from home for the first time.

Siri Sorenson felt that things were moving very slowly. If this was college, then it was one more thing in life not worth your full attention. After the dinner in Boston, she'd urged Sybele and "Don"—this was a first—to drive home early and skip Mass and the communion breakfast. When they dropped her off that night with a box of chocolates and

cookies from an ice-cream shop in Cambridge, Sybele in
tears, Siri walked in the dorm doorway and out again,
watching the brake lights of her father's car as it took the
curves of the tree-lined driveway. She had promised
Christo a call. He was staying with Teddy, although the
housekeeper would be there all day Sunday. She wouldn't
bother calling—the student union, where the phone booths
were private, might be closed for the night. Christo would
want to hear that she missed him and she loved him, but
she'd already said that dozens of times and it made no difference. They both knew that Siri was moving out of his
orbit. Whether she'd be back was up to her.

Upstairs, beyond the parade of toothbrushes and
bathrobes, past a card game in the smoker, and the proctor
(a senior—they'd been told—with a vocation) exiting her
room for bed-check, Siri found Esther digging into the
trunk, plunging her hand into the deepest section, under
the false floor, which Siri herself had packed before her
mother began laying in sweaters, coats and suits. All those
years spent defying the eyes and hands of an eager mother
and snooping brother had prepared Siri for this and more.
She shut the door and walked downstairs, paying a visit to
the third-floor lounge (shared by college and convent), fur-
nished with porch furniture and reading lamps. Only the
40-watt chandeliers were lit and the deep room was belted
in alluring shadows. Siri found a wide couch with its back
against the French doors. Old magazines—knitting, decorating, *Messenger of the Blind* and *Commonweal*—were scat-
tered on the glass-topped table and a floor ashtray was filled
with butts, although the lounge was not a smoker.

Upon her return, she found the dorm corridor deserted

and the proctor opening and shutting doors. Her own room was empty; the trunk was closed, covered by a lace runner from one of the dressers. Two bed pillows sleeved in the repulsive, shiny fabric were on top of that. The trunk had been dragged to a spot under the double window, softening the square symmetry of the room. (Next day Siri planned to speak to the dean of students and request a single.)

When Esther returned with a glass containing her toothbrush and -paste, a hand towel and cake of Ivory, she dumped these items on her bedspread and opened the bottom drawer of the roommate's dresser to show where she had put the wool sweaters. Then she moved the sweaters to show the flagon of Joy, filched from Siri's mother's bathroom, the package of Trojan safeties, the baby pictures, and—tucked in a shoebox—the Cherry Herring, Chartreuse, white rum and champagne.

Siri laughed at the neatness, but still planned to visit the dean. Even if Esther wanted to be friends, and could manage it, Siri needed privacy. This was her decision, made early in the summer before the first roommate letter had arrived. Before getting into bed—and after the proctor had knocked twice and flipped their light on and off—Esther, whose father had supplied the room with a carton of nickle Cokes, fixed two rum-colas in the toothpaste glasses. Siri took an aspirin with hers.

The talk that night was of food, boys, parents' ages and habits and favorite books. Siri didn't have a favorite, but offered *The Mill on the Floss,* which was on the senior-year reading list. Esther had read everything by George Eliot. "Who's George Eliot?" Siri asked, and "You're kidding,"

Esther replied, in a tone that gave Siri the needed clue. "Is the window open?" she said. "I'm freezing." Esther jumped up to check. No, but did she need an extra blanket? Yes, so a mothball-scented, scratchy cover, heavy as a door, fell on Siri's summer quilt. At first she felt smothered, but the weight and even the penetrating camphor were a refreshment in the night, when Siri felt incarcerated with a convent full of nuns just one floor down and beyond the wall. Mr. Sorenson was a non-Catholic and Siri was becoming one. She was more her father's daughter than her mother's, and that night she dreamed that she and Dad were married and living on a ship outside of China. The Chinese were smoking clove cigarettes until she kicked off the horse blanket and could breathe freely. "I hate it here," she told Esther Ferry when she woke up in the dark room and saw the roommate reading with a flashlight. "What time is it?"

At Mass and the endless communion breakfast, Siri was the only freshman to have shed the parents. Sybele's old friends, Martha and Judy, made room at their table, but Siri stayed with the Ferrys. Mrs. Ferry had on the same dress as yesterday and was still talking about the bedspreads, buying them "special" at a store where she didn't have a charge account and had to open one, so the girls had better make sure they liked them. They were not cheap. Then she asked if Siri planned to use the linen service or would she wash her own sheets, as Estie planned to do. This was not the kind of question Siri felt obliged to answer: it was nosy, it was none of this strange woman's business, it was boring and it didn't matter. Yes, she was enrolled in the weekly laundry service, but so what? She'd never made a bed in her life and didn't intend to start now, she'd already told Esther, who said: well, what about morning inspection? This question, too, had gone unanswered.

Mrs. Ferry talked on and without waiting for an answer or, just as often, answered her own questions, amplifying what Esther had already told her with hunches. Mr. Ferry said nothing. Esther listened carefully to all the deans and even to the alumnae who spoke after the eggy plates were cleared and fingerbowls supplied with squares of rich coffeecake. Later that day when the Ferrys had left, taking the ironing board and iron and lacy curtains and stepstool (clothespins and spray starch the girls didn't need or had no room to store), Esther told Siri what she had been listening for. In their opening remarks, "officials" tell you things they'll never say again, and if you don't take them in, you'll waste time—years maybe, your whole time here—puzzling out how things work. There's something they want you to know; it might not sound important but it is. Sometimes, Esther said, I write down what they say word for word.

On the basis of this and the restlessness that went with it, Siri decided not to visit the dean of students that Sunday. Her mother called on the floor telephone. Teddy wanted to talk, and so did Christo, who was still hanging around. Siri felt that she had important things to tell them if they only asked the right questions, but as she'd never before offered them anything, they didn't think to ask. And this obtuseness irritated her. Dad was on the extension and Mom on the kitchen phone. She could hear Teddy in the background. "I've got to go," she said. "Why? What do you have to do?"

said Sybele. "Study." "You haven't had classes yet," Dad said. "Placement tests," Siri said. "Placement in what?" Sybele asked. "In everything," Siri said. "Oh. Teddy wants to speak to you. And Christo."

"Speak up," she said into the receiver. "Girly girl," Teddy said.

"Is that all you have to say to me?"

"Hi, Siri Sue," Christo said.

"I've got to go now."

"Bye bye," said Teddy, then Christo had the phone to himself.

"Why are you still over there?" Siri asked him.

"I was babysitting Teddy."

"But why are you still there *now*?"

"How's college?"

"I don't know yet. I just got here."

"Are you coming home next weekend?"

"I don't know. I haven't even had my first class yet. Why don't you go home now?"

"Here's Teddy."

"Goony girl."

"I have nothing to say to you. Put Christo back on."

But when nothing happened, just childish breathing on the other end, Siri hung up. You could not use this phone to dial out—not that she wanted to talk to any of them ever again.

After one day of classes, Esther wanted to show Siri the pages she'd filled with opening remarks in math, chemistry,

History of the World and theology. Siri was also enrolled in History of the World, and had heard Dr. What'shisname's lecture herself. She remembered what Esther had said about the communion-breakfast speeches and had penciled in what she thought the history guy was driving at in his hour lecture: what is history? Siri had copied the outline from the board with its four headings: West, East, Ancient, Modern, with points under each, using numerals, numbers and letters. These were the best notes—and the clearest— she'd ever taken and she was proud to show them off. Just having Esther in the class, sitting in the front row near the teacher's desk, made it seem more interesting. Maybe Siri would major in history. It was all coming so easily for the first time. In the other classes: French and composition, sociology and Classics of Modern Literature, it was like high school: tedium, a blur of hard vocabulary words, demands and threats, all delivered in a brusque, mocking, bored and stilted—or otherwise hateful—tone. It was worse than high school because they (two men, one woman and one nun) talked faster with no stories or sidetracks, illustrations, jokes or personal remarks. Siri concentrated on her jewelry—a gold bangle and the signet ring from Albertus Magnus Prep. Tiny scratches spoiled the mirrory sheen of the bracelet. The delicate safety chain was already snapped and dangled, but it was eighteen-carat gold. Hollow. The ring was initialed and dated and Siri had it off and on, pushed onto the left and then the right hand. Her brother had wanted to buy her a graduation ring, but he had been prevented and it was too bad because two rings would balance two hands and set off the soft, pale fingers. Her mother said that he'd picked out an opal by himself—not anyone's favorite, but nicer than the black pearl, which was back in Christo's box. She'd get it from him when she went home, because she'd already promised it to Esther, the first time she'd offered anything of her own to anyone. "I'm not giving it to you, but you can wear it."

"I'll try to remember that," Esther had said, and Siri heard in it the mocking note that should give the clue, but this time didn't.

"So, show me," she said to Esther, who had a different-colored notebook for each subject. "No, let me show you first," she added. All her notes were in a ring binder—actually, there weren't any notes in the sections marked "Sociol," "Classics of," "Fr," "Compos."

She showed Esther the outline, "What Is History," and said, "You were in this class. I saw you up front."

Esther looked at the outline. "Oh," she said, "let me show you mine."

In Esther's blue notebook was:

"Arthur Donald Whitman (Harv. Ph.D., fourth year)

"European Intellectual History/Early Modern Europe/ Iberian Peninsula.

"Don't write. Listen. Don't comprehend. Read. At the end of every week, review your notes. Condense them. Abundance first, compression second. Boil everything down again before the midterm and final. If you organize too early, you'll lose the significant detail. Put it off too long and no organizational plan will contain it.

"Study is mental conditioning. Your minds are empty but tenacious; more avid and absorptive than they'll ever be again."

Siri read and of course once she did, she remembered,

but a wave of irritation flushed her cheeks. This was exactly the kind of thing she'd come to campus to avoid—lectures and scoldings and worst of all, the sickening sense that everything there was couldn't be seen and known in a glance. If there was more than met the eye, she didn't want to know about it. Life could be spoiled by this vague but threatening fringe which could seem like a world in itself. Esther wasn't afraid of the fringe: she was on the lookout for it. Siri wanted to say how ugly Esther's permanent was and how it made her mousy hair look like a bird's nest and how you could still smell the ammonia, especially when it was wet from the shower. Hair was something you could learn to manage if you were willing, and she and Sybele were: to put the time into it, to be patient and willing to sleep with pins and brush rollers pricking your scalp, or your ears burned by falling asleep with the dryer on. You could be electrocuted, strangle, suffocate and bleed to death, but when you woke up and unwound the hair, there was at least a day and a half of perfect results.

She could have told Esther this, but rules like this one were exactly what you couldn't explain, or even make notes about: you were like this or you weren't. If you were smart in this way, you learned automatically and you had your mother to help you. How could a mother like Esther's help her with anything?

All this Siri was thinking while Esther reread her own notes.

"Did you like him?" she asked.

"Who?"

"Mr. Whitman."

"Did *you?*"

"I wonder if he's married."

"Married! Who cares?" This line of thought (married) was worse than the stupid notes, the opinions of an older person irrelevant to them both. "I don't get you," Siri said, taking her own binder and putting it in a desk drawer where she'd stacked the new books purchased in the campus store. Esther had already asked to borrow the thick history text, a survey of the world from the beginning of time. Siri had never seen a book so huge with such small print. She refused to believe that between now and Christmas, they'd have to read half of it. Surely he couldn't mean every chapter, or if he did, there could be no reading expected in these other books which were also assigned for history. Sure, borrow it, Siri had said. Be my guest.

Siri had written her name in each new book. The look of the letters "Sorenson" made her homesick. Life here at St. Mary's wasn't as good as home, and it was supposed to be better. While she was writing her name—avoiding the temptation to make circles over the *is*—she was aware of Esther reading. In addition to what they had to buy for five classes, Esther had brought books of her own and she was finding the time to read them, in spite of the twenty pages of history assigned for tomorrow that should eat up all available reading time. Siri had started three conversations with Esther: Do you have any brothers and sisters? What did your school have—nuns or laypeople? And she already forgot the third, but in each case, Esther had answered (she had a brother; all lay), then gone back to the book. It felt creepy, worse than being alone, so Siri put all her books back in the drawer and picked up the August *Young Miss* she'd brought from home. "See you," said the roommate as Siri was closing the door. "Come and get me for dinner," Esther added without looking up.

That made Siri feel slightly better; there was continuity in it, although being stuck with someone like Esther (antisocial) for meal after meal was not what her magazine had counseled by way of getting the most out of freshman year, especially if you were stuck at an out-of-the-way, all girls school. That prospect made Siri resolve to scan the different checklists the magazine offered as tips for building an "outstanding" social life on campus. The rule she remembered was: Don't get tied down with the first person you meet. Don't form (she was sitting in the smoker with the magazine on her lap) any lasting attachments until you've been at least three times to the dining hall, the union, an all-school assembly and a dorm or student-council meeting. Look to upperclassmen for striking fashion forecasts as well as pointers on campus style. Attend classes, do your assignments on time, keep your grades up—these were on the "Scholastic" list—to avoid groundings, embarrassing failure and campus discipline. A waste of your time and your parents' money; or worse, a sign that college wasn't for you— a prospect so distasteful that the magazine writer didn't pursue it. *Young Miss* was a magazine for the "college-bound," which is what Siri had always been at Magnus Prep, and even before.

There were two girls in the smoker, one with a heating pad laid over her stomach and plugged into the wall. The other one had a patch of hair bleached nearly white and a gold disk with an elaborate monogram pinning her collar flat around her slender neck. She was holding a cupful of ice chips and the other girl was picking them out with her fingers. Siri noticed a resemblance, although the girl eating ice had straight brown hair with no streak. She asked them if they were twins and yes they were. What year? They were sophomores. Siri said she didn't know that sophomores had to live in the main house. We don't live here, they said. Siri waited, but they didn't say any more. "Are you sick?" she asked. "I'm dying," the plain twin said.

"Really?"

The pretty twin rolled her eyes. "You're a freshman, right?"

"That's a nice pin," Siri said. "I have one——"

But suddenly the plain twin got up and, holding her stomach, rushed out of the room. The pad fell off her lap and she nearly tripped on the wire. The pretty one followed. Siri stared at the heating pad, which was covered in soft flannel. Her heart was beating fast——it was the excitement of the emergency, but also of the unexpected contact with older girls. She couldn't concentrate on her magazine, but she didn't want to sit alone in the smoker doing nothing. If this girl (a twin) were pregnant, what did that mean?

In the dining hall Siri pointed out the twins to Esther. The roommates were sitting at a long table with girls from their end of the hall. Four out of eight had on Fair Isle sweaters, each a different heathered hue. Esther pointed this out to Siri as something funny, when Siri was just starting to feel at ease, almost as relaxed as she was at home. "What's wrong with that?" she said to Esther, hoping she remembered how many of that same kind of sweater had come out of Siri's new trunk. That was when the twins caught Siri's eye and did Esther think, Siri asked her, one of them looked sick, meaning pregnant? Esther looked and then turned to Siri. "I don't know. They look okay to me."

"I have their heating pad. They left it in the smoker."

"Are you going to keep it? I've got one."

"No. I'm giving it back. First I have to find out where they are." She paused. "Wouldn't you rather know sopho-mores than freshmen?"

"Why?"

"They're older."

"Not by much."

"I suppose," Siri said, with satisfaction at second-guess-ing this know-it-all, "you'd rather know the professors. The nuns! You'd rather know the nuns."

"Depends," said Esther. "I think I'd rather know Mr. Whitman, to start with, if you still think he's single."

"Who's Mr. Whitman?"

Two weeks later, when Siri woke up out of a deep sleep—and why she woke up was a mystery because she never did in her own bedroom where her mother had installed shades and drapes—she heard a noise so quiet, it was almost not there; you had to strain to hear, and if you strained that hard, you began to hear your own quiet sounds: air dredging out of a half-stuffed nose, the scratch of a rough nail on skin, or just tender skin against the starched sheets (and every day Siri's skin was getting drier

and more sensitive; she didn't have the right hand cream
and bought some cheap stuff at the campus store but could-
n't stand the smell of it: almonds, cherries, arsenic, so the
skin was nearly peeling from the shower soap: Dial—she
used whatever was in there, although Sybele had packed
two double cakes of Dove, and Siri had carried them all,
one by one, to the shower stalls and left them there, too
lazy or too stubborn [these were her main flaws, according
to her mother] to carry the soap cake back, wet and sticky,
to the room, and where would she put it? Leave it in the
bathroom and someone could take it, or let it drop to the
floor and melt over the drain. The soaps that didn't melt—
dark orange Dial or some industrial bar the school supplied
for sink use—were the only cakes available. Almost everyone else walked their soaps in a covered dish. Siri had one
but didn't like to touch the slippery, greasy thing, so she
took four showers in four days using a fresh, paper-
wrapped cake and let the wrapping drop to the shower-stall
floor and laid the oozy soap on the soap shelf. She felt she
was getting eczema, especially on the back of her legs, from
a combination of detergent soap, no hand cream, stiff towels and scratchy sheets.) It was unbearably itchy and maybe
it was that that woke her from the deep sleep she craved and
usually carved out ten or twelve hours from the night. It
was the reason—this volume of perfect sleep—that she had
such flawless skin and thick, shiny hair and beautiful, hard
nails with no ridges—or used to, before prison life started
drying her out, and now depriving her of an unbroken
sleep, and it was enough to make you cry, if someone else
weren't already crying.

"What's the matter?" Siri whispered in the dark. Esther didn't answer. Siri tried to sleep but the slight, slippery sounds kept her alert. Even with the pillow over her head, she could hear. Then Esther got up, picked up her robe from the floor where she'd dropped it—Siri dropped hers there too—and left. The corridor light sliced into the room. Siri felt as if she'd been shot. She wanted to cry, too, but was too dried out to produce even a moistening over the eyeballs. The relentless process, starting here and continuing until her skin was a road map of scaly, rough redness, brought to her head a sudden warmth of salty water and soon she was crying as hard as Esther, but fell asleep before the roommate returned and could tell her story.

When Siri woke that morning, her face waxy from the night cry and runny nose, Esther was gone again; her bed was made and the floor stripped of clothes. The clock said that half of the first class—Siri couldn't remember whether it was sociology or "Classics of Modern"—was over. She knew the day started in the basement in room 02, and next was 22 on the first floor, but which was first and already half over, she couldn't recall. She was starving and thirsty and a little tired and too dry to take another shower, so she decided to sleep. At eleven thirty, when every scrap of sleep lost in the night had been redeemed, with a surplus, she got up, and borrowing Esther's straw slippers, scuffed to the bathroom, forgetting her towel, so having to dry her face with paper. At least the stickiness was rinsed off. Her hair needed washing, but there was no time. The corridor was empty and so was the bathroom. Siri found a corduroy dress and matching knee socks and a pair of flats. She had brought a dozen pairs of these flats but only wore the navy blue ones because they went with everything and were all broken in, soft as gloves, so loose you could step right out of them.

She watched out the window for a sign of girls exiting the last period. Every student had three morning periods, a nine, a ten and an eleven. At two o'clock the periods started again and most students had a two, a three and a four, with dinner at five. Esther was taking six subjects, so busy all day. She came back to the room at a little before five to meet Siri, who rested or read a magazine or listened to the radio until supper. After supper, Esther went to the library. At ten she came back to the room, and by eleven, the proctor came by for room check. It was an easy schedule to remember, easier than high school, and Siri felt that she'd made a quick and lasting adjustment, although she still didn't know where anything was. The campus was a maze of paths and same-looking buildings.

She watched until the girls from the basement classes came surging out the side door, then ran down the staircase to melt into the crowd.

She didn't see Esther or any of their corridor mates until she had filled a tray. They were all at the end of the line as usual because they were teacher's pets and liked to talk after class. Siri put her tray down and waved. The dining hall was deafening at noon—screams, silverware, the din of the kitchen, the slamming of huge, metal food lids on the service line. Siri had never seen food laid out this way: tubs of stringy green and oily orange and a hill of boiled potatoes, skin all crusty and full of gritty eyes; bleeding meats and bowls full of icy sauces and jugs of hot fudge and vanilla pudding; Jello cubes, canisters of mustard and a wall of milk: chocolate, skimmed and coffee cream, along with fruit punch and orange-pineapple juice. Every lunch there was fruit cocktail in cut-glass bowls. If you found nothing you liked, there was a jumbo loaf of white bread spilling its slices next to a bowl of peanut butter and a tank of jam. The dining hall often smelled of fish or curdled milk—if not, then burnt toast and reheated coffee. It was just as well to have a stuffed-up nose and a pack of Juicy Fruit and keep your cigs close at hand. Some girls slipped out every fifteen minutes for a butt and came back with a headful or a sweaterful of pungent smoke. That and cologne or Jean Naté and you could be out before any of the food smells had soaked through.

By the time Esther arrived at the table, Siri had finished her lunch. On her tray was a complete bread crust like a frame; inside the frame were the mushrooms and peppers she had picked out of today's omelet. Since she hadn't had breakfast or dinner the night before, she had also nibbled the top of a muffin—the part she was sure was cooked. She had no appetite for this food, but lunch was the easiest to choke down.

"Hi, Room," Esther said. "Where were you this morning?"

"Where were *you*?"

"I was in class where you should have been."

"I mean last night," said Siri, drinking a little of the blend Esther liked to mix of juice and jello. It was lumpy but usually tasted good.

Esther didn't answer. She pointed to a mouthful of egg salad and kept chewing. Seeing egg salad galore on everyone's plate made the reality of the day (meatless) dawn on Siri. It was Friday. It was the date of the first college mixer.

"I couldn't sleep," said Esther, after a swallow of the Jello-juice mixture.

"Was that you I heard crying?" Siri asked.

Esther didn't answer, but the look she gave was clearly meant to communicate something. Was Esther sad? Siri felt she knew Esther as well—or better—than she knew her family or Irene, but Esther kept showing a different side. When Siri tried to add it all up, it didn't. Siri hated a mystery; but there were parts of Esther she liked and they were—for the time being—stuck with each other. Before Siri even got the chance to make an appointment with the dean of students (a big, chunky nun with a fake-looking smile), the freshmen were told there were to be no room changes until the new year. Siri had, in any case, come to depend on Esther. It was Esther who woke her up in the morning, who cleaned up the room in time for inspection, who offered to help with history assignments, if Siri needed it (so far she didn't, but it was good insurance; in fact, just knowing Esther was there made Siri relax about all her class work; Esther was a genius; the girls on their floor already knew it. And they didn't—this was the surprise—hate her or make fun of her behind her back. Esther's oddities were well tolerated. She had even been elected floor representative). Everything was working out.

"If you have something on your mind, you can talk to me," Siri said. "I can keep a secret," she added.

Esther snorted, but didn't say anything rude. Before she was fully aware of it, Siri realized she was expecting a rude remark. Maybe Esther had that kind of a face: critical or negative. Actually, Esther had a friendly face, wide with eyes half closed and a big, stretchy mouth. Her face looked serious some of the time, but never mean.

"Tell me about Irene," Esther said, out of the blue, changing the subject, as she often did.

"What about her?"

"Is she ever going to come and visit?"

"You mean—in Rick's car, with Rick?"

"With Rick, sure, and the guy you were seeing."

"Christo? We broke up."

"When did that happen?"

"A couple of days ago. Last week sometime. He brought it up."

"Really?"

"All he was doing was waiting around. It wasn't fair."

"Are Rick and Irene still getting married?"

"I guess so."

"Do you miss seeing them all the time?"

Siri reflected. She wasn't sure how to answer this. She didn't really miss any of the home people. It was as if she'd never lived there, or gone to high school, or babysat for Teddy.

"You don't! I can see it. It won't last. It's the novelty of a new place," Esther said, as if she could read Siri's mind, which was the case sometimes, and was another thing Siri came to depend upon. Sometimes Esther knew what Siri was thinking before Siri was finished thinking. Esther was speeding things up and that was fun, when it wasn't sickeningly head-spinning.

Irene had been Siri's best friend since seventh grade and before that, Siri was best friends with Louise Eder, but neither of them (or Christo either) could figure out what she was thinking before she thought it, and she wouldn't have dreamt of depending on them for that.

"So why were you crying?" she asked Esther, as they walked back to their room.

"How am I supposed to answer a question like that?" said Esther, stopping short on the gravel path. Siri was already bored with this daily tracking—caf to dorm, dorm to caf. It was enough to make you scream, and this was only the first month.

"Why don't you just tell the truth." This statement popped out of Siri's mouth; it was the kind of nervy remark Esther would make—already had made a billion times.

Esther laughed. "The truth. You sound like a five-year-old. Hey, you never told me if that twin you like so much is really pregnant. Did you ask her?"

"I don't know her. Her sister says she's okay."

"Are you going to your afternoon classes?"

"Why wouldn't I? Are you?"

"I haven't missed one so far."

Siri stopped on the path in front of the dorm. "Congratulations."

"Hey! You made a joke," Esther said. "See you in history. I'll save you a seat."

And Esther would, but Siri was never there early enough to take a seat so close to the front.

Siri checked her mailbox and found another "urgent" reminder to call her mother. Sybele called every other day, but half the time Siri told "Phone Duty" to say she wasn't there. Sometimes Sybele would ask to speak to Esther. "Esther, dear," she'd croon, and Esther could imitate her to a flaw, "please tell my daughter——." Just the snotty way she said "daughter" and not "Siri" reminded Esther of the thing over the bedspreads. Esther had decided that instant not to move into Honor's House where she was supposed to be with the other merit scholars, but to stick with Siri. She hadn't expected to like her, but she did, kind of. And together they went to war with Sybele. For reducing Esther's poor mother to a cinder in one second, Esther still planned to return the favor.

Siri discarded the pink telephone slip. At home she had been Sybele's only friend and ally——not counting Teddy, who didn't count. Dad stayed out of the way. He blamed it on the smoking but everyone knew that if it weren't the cigarettes, it'd be something else, some other way to stay locked up in his garage studio or hammering duck heads on the breezeway. Sybele liked to say that they were like twins, Sybele and Siri, but they weren't. Sybele was heavy and Siri light; Sybele was a redhead (dyed) and Siri a blond. Everything in Sybele's closet was black for its slimming effect, or white for coolness. Siri liked colors and nothing dark.

Siri never called back, but once in a blue moon would allow Phone Duty to reach her. As soon as the receiver was in contact with her head, she'd be shouting or sneering, silent and sulky. "How can you speak to me this way!" Sybele would wail.

Mrs. Ferry rarely called and it was always Esther's father who did the dialing and spoke to Phone Duty, using most of the three minutes before the egg timer went off. But she sent packages. Inside a box from a department store that had gone out of business after the war (Esther explained that her mother never threw anything out, not old magazines, not paper bags, not even ancient pots and pans) were nests made of newspaper: hard candy in one, three tangerines or a handful of nuts, something handmade and housewifely (potholders, set of doilies, a new tape measure), religious articles (a rosary made of beans from some equatorial mission, a bottle of holy water, church reminders), clothing (mostly underwear bought at sales: panties and garter belts and half slips); occasionally a five-dollar bill and a roll of quarters for laundry; something fresh baked but already stale and crumbly (date bars, white fudge, banana bread). Esther tossed the food, paper goods and clothing, but kept all the homemade gifts. They were destined for fireman's funds and Christmas bazaars, or the Salvation Army. The money was put to immediate use. She'd borrowed cash from Siri for books and typewriter ribbons, soap and shampoo, subway fare to Boston.

That afternoon, Siri attended both the 2 and the 3; they were in her building and easy to get to. Her mind was on the mixer and the effort of sorting her best skirts and sweaters, blouses and dresses to come up with the perfect outfit (she knew how to dress for boys). Every detail was planned down to the underwear, tights and stacked heels, and she was already dancing, one of the first freshmen to be picked on the darkened floor of the union, to join the cute twin and a few seniors pinned to Harvard boys, when she heard her name called out in a different room, and the sound of her own voice saying, "I lost my place. I'm sorry," and it could have been tenth grade at Magnus or fifth grade at St. Charles Borromeo. That's how it felt to be singled out in front of all these staring strangers.

She felt the disgusting omelet curdling in her stomach. She could taste the catsup. In a minute the sudden appearance of that lunch would bring this class to a halt if this nun—or whoever it was—kept insisting that she find her place, and answer the question. The miracle was the girl across the aisle spilling it out—whatever it was the teacher was asking and—except for the look Siri was getting and the note dropped on her desk, when an in-class assignment of verbs began—the problem was solved.

The hateful thing was that the shock of it, the physical reaction, had obliterated all memory of the carefully selected outfit and accessories, so she had to start all over again, and the pleasure of it destroyed. Thoughts of the mixer brought nothing but a sense of tedium and shame. Siri wanted to go home; she wanted to curl up on her own quilt in her own room and die in her sleep.

During the last fifteen minutes of the 3 o'clock, she lay her head on the desk and did sleep. After that, a trip to the infirmary, where she drank a warm Coke and swallowed two aspirins.

Esther was "in a panic," as she said, when it was 5 and 5:15 and no Siri. But here she was, and rather than stand in line, why not skip dinner, which they did, and made up for it with a package of snowballs (Esther) and a Snickers (Siri) and weak, machine coffee in the snack bar. It was exciting to be the only ones there, listening to the hubbub of the dining hall over their heads. "I don't want you to get thrown out," Esther said, when Siri said what had happened, and Siri was grateful, but that was not even a remote possibility, and for the first time she mentioned what she was never to mention (according to Dad's single piece of advice to his only daughter), the fact that the Stevensons (Sybele's mother and aunts) had built the student union and the school chapel and were the first names listed in the "Order of St. Mary, Lifetime Friends," which is how Siri, with the grades she got in high school, had gotten in in the first place.

After that, Esther called Siri the "special student" and her program "special ed." And even though Siri would never have thought of looking at it that way—and Sybele wouldn't be pleased to hear it said about the Stevensons or her only daughter—it had its good side: it made Siri less worried about college; somehow it seemed more personal: she could count on people (faculty included) as she'd counted on Sybele and Dad, and even Irene and Christo. People were looking out for her in a way that they weren't and never would look out for Esther, or even the brilliant, single (Esther knew) Mr. Whitman, who was making education his business, something Siri felt she'd never understand, especially now that she could see—through Esther's vivid words—what a hunk he was, looked a lot like Dad.

And he lived near campus! This was the shock they got that night when, arriving late for the mixer, there he was in a sleeveless sweater and knitted tie, serving as a bodyguard (Siri), chaperone (Esther corrected). He was leaning up against a bulletin board and Esther thought they should approach him immediately. Go yourself, Siri said. She wasn't going to waste valuable time—little enough of it allotted for meeting boys their own age—on a "fruitcake" (a word Irene used for guys she considered too old to be taken seriously, yet not easy to shake off). Esther seemed shy about confronting the teacher alone, and she settled for anchoring a free-standing column, well sited for notice, yet a graceful spot, part in shadow, near the refreshment booth.

There they stood. Siri had fixed up Esther who—now that she'd lent her decent clothes and trimmed the frizzy ends of the perm, and offered her own soft-hued cosmetics for the stuff Esther brought (cake rouge and an eyebrow pencil; an old lipstick, more black than red)—looked okay, off to one side, and angled. This was not just to show Esther at her best, in profile, with stomach sucked in, but left most of the good light (the bad light was coming from the refreshment booth and beyond: a block of glary fluorescence) for Siri to stand in, facing out, with her eyes on the doorway. Esther tried to rotate, but Siri's hand, clasping her arm ("Stay put!"), rotated her back. Esther didn't need to look. Siri would fish out the best, better than anything Esther could dream of hooking. Esther seemed to know it too because, after one correction, she stayed in place, sheltered near the cornsilk blond in rose pink sweater and skirt, a human magnet.

It was not a question—Esther still didn't understand this—of whether they'd be asked to dance, but of how many partners they could collect and fob off, and whether it could be done fast enough to single out some takers before the band took a break. Siri had in her shoulder bag the bottle of Cherry Herring, but it was for after. She counted on these boys from St. Ambrose to be swift enough to furnish their own and share it.

And what happened but Esther ended up with Mr. Whitman, after all. The minute Siri left the column to dance with what turned out to be a junior oarsman from BU, already drunk and pouring hot breath over Siri's powdered neck, who tried to pass her off to his frat brother for half of the slow dance, but no thank you, Esther was gone. Coming back from the ladies' room where she cooled her neck with a wet hand towel, Siri saw how young she looked— not at all like Irene's sophisticated girlfriend, so superior to a child like Christo. She was flushed from the dance and the standing and being pawed by the ape from BU. Her makeup did not darken or intensify her blue eyes or make her little nose and rosebud mouth look more mature than a baby's. Her cheeks were fatter and whatever she thought—earlier in the evening, while making up Esther's sallow face—she was bringing to this dance was not what she saw in the mirror, even compared to the other freshmen, who flitted in and out of sight, teasing their hair or blotting an oily nose.

It was discouraging. And when she came out, no Esther. She was not on the dance floor, or buying a Coke. Before the same smirky jock could bother Siri again (she could see him heading her way), she spotted Esther in a clump of girls talking to Mr. Whitman. There was nothing to do but join them; the night was already spoiled. But en route, a sandy-haired beanpole with glasses stopped her and asked if she were some other name: Trudy something. She could feel her face tightening. "Would you like to dance anyway?" the loser asked. And, as she had nothing better to do, she let it happen, and happen again. Every question he asked, she answered with one word or less. He didn't seem to care, as long as she kept dancing, and as she still had nothing better to do, she did. And the miracle happened then: *he* cut in. At first, the beanpole wasn't going to give way, but Siri had already squirmed out of his grasp and was aiming herself toward her future husband.

For the first time in her life, roped inside this guy's muscular arms, Siri wished she had something to say, but even if she had, she presently lacked the breath to say it. Even then, in heaven, as it were, she was looking sideways for Esther, to help or to admire, and angering to think that just now, when she was needed, Esther was deaf and blind to anything but Mr. Whitman. This fabulous-looking boy (dark curls, big teeth, ten feet tall) didn't ask any question, or offer conversation. His grip on Siri and his rhythmic motion (he had gone to dancing class: the difference was clear) were what he had to give. They danced and they danced again. By the third dance, Siri could feel something like a hand grenade being pressed on her. She knew what it might be, but refused to think that someone she hardly knew could be so brazen, the nerve of it! She inhaled and tried to suck the front of her body into her spine, but still the grenade or bean bag pressed just below the waistband of her skirt. And now I'm in for it, she thought, as life began to conform into something more like what it was for other people (Irene, for instance, or even Sybele): painful, stupid, a drag.

There, though—finally!—was Esther. She was back near the column with her eyes glued on Siri. Did she see? Not only did she see, but striding onto the dance floor with no excuse or partner, tapped the thug's shoulder, saying: "She has a phone call. She's got to come take it." And the surprise of it hit him too, and he relaxed his grip. By then, Siri was in tears and the whole room knew something was up, but what exactly happened, they never knew for sure— not even Esther. "He was taking advantage of you, wasn't he?" was all she said, and that made Siri cry harder, although she was sure Esther, a baby, didn't know: no one, who wasn't there to feel it, could really know.

Soon after in real time, but what seemed to Siri like at least a year later, they were all sitting around a table, with Mr. Whitman offering to buy her a Coke. He was kind to Siri. He recognized her from his class, but didn't treat her like a dumbbell or a goof-off, the main reason she avoided teachers and most adults. She sat there, tuning out their talk and the music, and studied her puffy fingers and the gold bracelet.

That night she called home, but when her mother offered to drive out to get her the next day, she said no, knowing (a first) that if she went home and slept one night under her canopy in her own bedroom, she'd never come back. She had to fight with both parents, and yell insulting things at Sybele until she hung up, still crying, but Siri would stay. How long? Until SMC was finished with her, or she with it, whichever came first. And the thought—brave, reckless even—was dazzling.

2.

But the family came anyway—at least Sybele and Teddy did. When they arrived, Great Hall was empty, for the noon Mass drew out the college and "the community," as the nuns called themselves. No one was at the switchboard, so Sybele sent Teddy up to reconnoiter. She had assumed—as had Teddy—that Siri was still asleep. Teddy had brought his sister five of his best comic books, a penknife and a silver whistle. She could keep them—they might come in handy. He had shown his mother the presents and discussed their timeliness, which is how Sybele knew he knew something had happened, but she didn't care to explore the subject of sex with someone so young, although Donald didn't want to get into it either. She'd like to blame him, such an inattentive and uninvolved dad— especially with their oldest—but since Siri's move to St. M's, Donald had seemed even more remote. Things were peaceful with no sulks or sudden outbursts and slamming of doors, but Siri was the one who drew her father out, who could involve him when nothing else could. Donald was the kind who should never have married and had a family, Sybele thought, eyes tearing as she recalled her mother's on-the-spot assessment.

Five minutes later, Teddy was back—no one up there

either. Did he know the room number? Sybele asked. Do you? he said. Since neither of them knew the number (Sybele had seen the room, but couldn't remember which end of the corridor), they'd have to wait. The chapel was connected to Great Hall, but on the convent side. When the Sorensons heard the sudden bleat of the organ, making them jump, they knew the Mass was over.

Sybele recognized Esther, although the girl looked different. Teddy noticed she had his sister's corduroy jumper on, because there was the monogram, the triple S.

Teddy was introduced to Esther and already giddy from the nearness of these clean, glossy girls. The fourth floor had gathered to see whose mother this was and Sybele was glad she had worn her best suit. And here was Sister, the dean of students, who didn't seem to know anything, so Sybele shook hands and presented her boy, acting as if nothing but the pleasure of the trip had brought them there so soon after school had started. Sister invited them (Where *was* Siri? she asked and Esther and Sybele talked over each other. "Sick," Teddy said and the nun's face slumped in sympathy) for a collation in the convent dining room. Sybele said they didn't quite have time, but thank you.

Sybele, Teddy and Esther parading in after Mass was exactly what Siri didn't want to see after the night she'd spent. The bedclothes were all knotted. A patchwork of lurid dreams had erased the dance, but the dance came back as soon as Esther started clattering around getting ready for Mass. Things looked different in the light of day, which is why Siri hated mornings. Last night's adventure had been thrilling—and it could still be thrilling. Was that boy thinking of her right now? If he was thinking, what was he thinking? This was exactly the question that needed the darkness to bear fruit. And the room was still dark, but here was the family and Esther, barging in. They knew what they knew, but what they knew had no connection with the things going on in her head. Siri knew something that she'd never tell them, or at least not today: she was in love.

In the glare of Sybele's questions and the harassing presence of Teddy and Esther, who sometimes supplied answers to the questions, the love blossomed. Siri took great pains to put a face to her love. She'd had four dance partners in all and the face she singled out had a trait borrowed from each. There was no voice yet, no words. Even the suffocating bearhug, so amazing at the time, was now indistinguishable from the oarsman's grip—his ropey arms and padded back. Boys had these similarities which made out of their totality a bare handful of types: there was the monkey type, like Christo, the oarsman, the brainy beanpole and the Humpty Dumpty. Most of the old ones were Humpters, except maybe Dad, who still had a little oarsman in him and who was heading toward a sexless state like Christo's. Siri didn't want a mate like that, now or ever.

Taking her daughter aside, Sybele wanted to know if she needed to see a doctor.

"For what?"

Esther said it wasn't necessary and was told on the spot to please take Teddy and wait outside by their car. Sybele was treating everyone to brunch, but first had to speak privately to Siri, who then had to get herself dressed.

"Don't go," Siri told Esther, but Teddy was already swinging on the doorknob, dragging his knees along the splintery floor, so out, out!

"Tell me again what happened," Sybele said, as soon as the door was closed.

But Siri now had a different story from the one her mother knew, so "don't ask me!" she said.

"Come sit on my lap," Sybele said, "and be my baby girl," and Siri did, resting her head on her mother's fat shoulder.

"Look at me," Sybele said, and at first, Siri wouldn't, but then, feeling the story taking firm shape with a deep and unshakable root (joining a couple of other life stories she had created), she let her eyes rest on her mother's.

"Tell me," Sybele pleaded.

Siri sighed, but didn't blink.

"All right," the mother said, "be a stubborn mule. If that's the thanks I get for driving all the way out here, I guess that's the thanks I get."

This lame remark made Siri smile and a smile from Siri, unprompted, was always a treat. Sybele kissed her daughter, a college girl and already maturing, and helped her pick out something pretty to wear. Siri showered and checked her flat belly for any outline the boy might have left, but found only smoothness. She pinched the skin till it stung and produced a moon-shaped welt.

At brunch, Esther was seeing Sybele in a new light and wishing she could be someone else's mother. Sybele had much to offer on this migraine-free day and Siri, self-sufficient and now more so, had no use for the praise, adoring looks and promises of a new this and that and trips here and there to buy it.

"How did you two," Teddy said, because no one was paying attention to him, "get to be girlfriends?"

"Teddy," Sybele said. "Don't be so rude, and please use your napkin."

Teddy, who had been sipping his sister's over-sugared coffee, took his napkin in his teeth.

"I'm warning you!" his mother said.

"Leave him alone," Siri said, peering at the boy's uninteresting face (almost a non-face) to see what he had absorbed from this brunch. He was usually absorbing something, but didn't always say what it was. He was clearly showing off for Esther's sake, so Siri looked at her. In four weeks' time, Esther was a different person from the kinky-haired mole Siri had met standing barefoot on the braided rug Siri had long since tossed out their window, then made Esther drag to the laundry room, where it was instantly filched. Esther's hair was shiny now that she used shampoo, not hand soap; and cut better, even though an amateur job. Her skin was less blotchy since Siri had trashed the Phisohex in its hideous green bottle. The girl had one decent skirt which she wore every day, once Siri had pointed out what was wrong (everything) with the others, and borrowed Siri's sweaters, shoes, tights, makeup, hairbrush, hairdryer and rollers. She was still mousy, but other girls had noticed an improvement and the type naturally drawn to someone like Siri would be less put off by this new Esther. She was still a bookworm, a drone, a wallflower, teacher's pet, goody-good and stick-in-the-mud, but—Siri glanced at her keen-eyed brother—even Teddy had no trouble pairing them together, and he could spot a discrepancy from a mile away. There was sarcasm in his remark, or maybe it was the goony word "girlfriends." Siri was getting touchy about words, things she'd never noticed before or cared two cents about.

"Girlfriends" seemed like something from "Betty and Veronica," or out of Irene's life, now that she and Joan Hendricks, operators, double-dated, according to the only letter Siri had received (beside Dad's bird postcards). Irene had girlfriends, but Esther didn't—and Siri would never, if she could help it.

But now she was in love and almost a different person. She closed her eyes to shut out the sight of that inquisitive, brotherly face. When she said the words "in love," she was more in love. What would it be like to be married to—. Siri didn't know his name, and the right name for that type of guy didn't spring to mind. She didn't want Esther to name him, and Esther had been on the verge of doing it.

Teddy shared an eclair with Esther, who was supposed to avoid anything chocolate for the sake of her complexion; Sybele had a bowl of raspberry-lime sherbet and Siri ordered black coffee—a fresh cup, which she would drink without the half-and-half and sugar cubes. It seemed right for the mood: bitter, hot, so hot it brought tears to the eyes, and the need for a smoke. Trying to quit, Sybele had brought no cigarettes, but bought a pack and let Siri pick the brand: Kools.

To get the black coffee down she scooped ("Hey!") chocolate icing from the top of Teddy's half eclair.

"Hay is for horses," scolded Sybele, passing her sherbet to Siri, who passed it back.

"Don't be a brat," Sybele said.

"Don't be immature," Siri said.

"Don't speak to your mother that way."

"Don't speak to *me* that way!"

"That's enough."

Throughout dessert and coffee, Esther had kept her eyes on Mrs. Sorenson's face. Not a beautiful face and probably never had been, but the ivory skin and eyes the color of blue marbles, the smooth hair (red, but an up-to-date red, not the blackish orange of Mrs. Ferry's friends who dyed their hair) reminded Esther of Renoir. There was no tension or much expressiveness in the face and that, too, made it easier to look at than Esther's mother's face. (When she had tried to call her mother "Anna," she found it no improvement over "Mrs." or "Ma." Nothing in Anna Ferry's name, self or story made her youthful. Why was that?)

Do you love your parents? Esther had asked Siri their first night as roommates.

What? Siri had said, long before Esther knew that she never answered a direct question.

She didn't answer questions and didn't ask them, but if she did, "no" was the only answer Siri would believe, having seen Esther's parents with her own eyes.

When Sybele and Teddy brought Siri and her roommate back, it was Sunday afternoon, the worst hours of the worst

day of the week. The car filled with glum silence. Even
Teddy, anticipating his own girl-free house and a father
with hours alone to remove himself still further from his
family, and the sparks that could fly when Mum reentered
that bachelor zone with wooden birds resting on their dusty
straw, a jelly jar of whiskey-Coke and an old jazz record still
spinning on the hifi, had folded himself into his own corner
and was nibbling his jacket lapel—off to the side where no
one could see. Teddy hated the college, and if his eyes had
been flamethrowers, all these blazing red and yellow trees
lining the driveway would be blasted, the blacktop cracked
and gutted, and that happy house or great house—whatever it was—burned to the ground. Both of these girls
could sleep at his house—Teddy had the extra twin bed in
his room for Esther. Why was his family busting up just
because of stupid college?

And here they were at the doorway, kisses and hugs, and
Siri snapping her fingers under his nose, reminding him that
he had nothing to call his own, not even this sister and her
roommate, who already had her back to him, looking at
Sybele, who was looking at Siri, who was already at the
door and slamming it in their face. She was still immature,
his sister, but she was what he had, as he reminded his
mother on the way home, when she ranted and scolded,
and even cried a little. "You've got me," she said, and that
soothed him, and proved his mother was growing up.

Nothing could soothe Siri, who hadn't cracked a book in
a week and was too deflated to start now after an exhaust-
ing weekend and a wasted day. She crawled into her

unmade bed, kicking out her sweater and skirt onto the floor. "And don't pick them up," she said to Esther.

"I wasn't going to," Esther said, stretching a rubber band around a ponytail—"the Samurai," Siri called her, now that she knew what a samurai was, or had at least seen a movie called samurai-something, black and white and boring, but now she knew the word.

Usually, if she learned a new word, she forgot an old one, or one that sounded the same. College was slowly replacing the stock of home words with jumbo words that had no real meaning, useless, but still capable of driving out the familiar phrases from home—some of them Teddy's, some Dad's. Siri closed her eyes. She remembered with the first words that came to mind ("garter belt") that she was in love. (No one wore garter belts anymore—she was almost asleep now—everyone needed "support." Where did the bulge go, once all this support pushed it in?)

"How long are you going to study?" she forced herself to say to Esther, even though she had to wake up to do it.

"I just got started."

"So, how long?"

"As long as it takes me to finish."

"Hurry up."

"I'll wake you when I'm done."

"Don't forget."

Esther was reading *Madame Bovary* out loud, and to Siri it was just like a home movie, parts about Esther's family (the husband, the farm), and sometimes Siri's (Emma, the beautiful clothes, all the love affairs after Leon). It was becoming the best part of a good day and relief after a lousy day like today.

"This could happen to you," Esther had said when she started. "This book shows the value of an education, which Emma didn't have."

Siri couldn't see that the novel had the least connection to education, but she could see the similarities between herself and Emma. Something bad was going to happen to this girl, and Siri was dreading it. She didn't mention the dread to Esther because Esther knew the whole story and might spill the beans. Siri was a slow reader, but Esther was fast. If Siri fell asleep before Esther had finished a chapter, Siri reread the whole chapter by herself, no matter how long it took. This was a story she wanted to hear.

But Esther never woke her that Sunday night, because she fell asleep studying, and then was too tired to do more than roll into bed. She didn't even turn out the light.

Two months into the term, right after Thanksgiving, Siri woke twice in one week to the sound of crying. The first time she managed to get back to sleep. Next day she remembered, but forgot to ask when she saw Esther that night for supper. Siri was attending some of the classes and had only failed one subject in midterms, and that was because the test was completely unfair and she had bad cramps. After a conference with the dean, the teacher agreed to strike the F from the grade book and to give the girl extra help before the final. The head nun was pleased with Sorenson's progress: the record was better than anyone could have hoped, and there was room for slippage. She might even make it through freshman year.

The second time, Siri was not asleep when the crying started, and when it got louder and more upsetting, there was nothing to do but get up and snap on the light.

"Turn it off!" Esther said, and—for the first time in her life—Siri took an order. "Tell me why you're crying," she said.

"I'll tell you tomorrow."

"Tell me tonight, or I'll turn the light back on."

"You don't want to hear," said Esther, her voice soaked with tears.

Siri gave her a minute, and asked again. Danny, Esther's older brother—he was ten years older, and like a father to Esther—had gone into the seminary in eighth grade.

"I thought you were an only child," said Siri, also thinking that yes, maybe she didn't want to hear this.

Well, Danny left the seminary a year before he was set to be ordained. Instead of becoming a priest like they all expected and—in the case of her mother and father—were living for, he got married. And now he and Cynthia had two boys. But—and here Esther was swamped again.

"Yeah? So?" Siri said.

Well, if that weren't bad enough—and it was bad because if anyone had a vocation, it was Danny: the seminary was his whole life—now he was alcoholic. The trouble was he liked to drink. Most priests do, and it was one of the few things they could do in the seminary, especially when they were sent over to Europe, as Danny was, where people drink wine all day long.

Esther liked Danny's wife, the whole family liked her—that wasn't the problem. Cynthia was a nurse, but Danny wasn't very happy in the marriage.

"So, he drinks?"

"He's an alcoholic. So, if he drinks, he blacks out, and if

he blacks out, he gets into trouble. The cops took his license away, then he lost his job."

Esther was crying again.

"How do you know?"

"My father told me."

He sounded like a loser, Siri wanted to say, but Esther probably knew that already, and people didn't like you to badmouth their family, even if they did it first.

"Thanks for listening," Esther said. "It's not your problem."

It sure wasn't! Siri was thinking—her Dad wasn't even a Catholic and Teddy would never go into a seminary. They could hardly get him to go to school. "Are you going to be okay?" she asked. "I'm falling asleep."

It was wonderful to escape into sleep, to dive down that dark hole; but the walls of the hole were getting thinner and light was squeezing through. Why was this happening? It was because of college: college wasn't what people thought. Siri was having her first idea, lying there listening to Esther's snaggled breathing, which could make her mad enough to kill Esther, or at least smack her, but as with everything else, she was getting used to the pitiful sounds. They used the word "vulnerable" in classes. Siri didn't know what it meant, but she knew it was bad, not something she wanted to try to be. That snagged breathing seemed vulnerable, if vulnerable meant poor and without a future. Oddly, Esther seemed to think she had one. That made her more vulnerable.

College, Siri was thinking, could take a solid person like herself, who slept well and had no fears and was far from vulnerable, with a pretty face, good skin, size nine or even seven, and punch holes in the solidness. What did the punching was all the thinking they forced you to do if you were going to pass your courses. It was hard to do, but just as it became easier, it began to hurt you. This was the kind of thought Esther would be interested in, but Esther needed her sleep even more Siri. Esther was always tired. She woke up tired and was often too tired—after studying all day, and reading and thinking—to sleep, so she did more study-ing. Esther had been to the nurse, who prescribed a hot shower and quiet time, and Siri had recommended a little nip before falling into bed.

It seemed to be working, at least for Esther. Siri, who came to college needing eight or nine unbroken hours a night, now slept only half the night. She was groggy all morning, but went to her classes anyway. It was better than being stuck in the room by herself, then slinking around trying to avoid teachers.

They wanted you to think around the clock, in class and out, and Siri found the thinking slopping over into the night, even after a full chapter of *Madame Bovary,* which she was liking less, and liking Emma less as she was getting to know her better, and as the thing she was dreading got closer. Dates could be spoiled. At the second mixer, Siri had exchanged names and PO boxes with a boy from MIT. He had a car and they drove one Sunday into town to see the Christmas lights. The boy was just a date, no great shakes (cute face, but short and stocky), walked Siri through the Common and the Public Gardens, then down Boylston Street to Copley Square, talking the whole time. Siri had never heard a boy chatter like this. Christo would talk—but only if he had a project (he was always building something), or his feelings were hurt, and then he'd say just enough and they could go back to miniature golf or eating a sundae or watching TV. This boy, Terry his name was, had never spent time in a big city like Boston. He was interested in everything—art museums, old statues, politics, movies and foreign countries. He was a chemistry major and planned to go into the foreign service or be a psychiatrist. He wanted to know Siri's major and she made one up: sociology, the course she'd failed, and the stupidest subject she'd ever heard of, and had only taken because it fit the time slot and you were supposed to try new things in college. Terry seemed impressed. Luckily, they had to cross a busy street before he could rattle off the dozen questions he was thinking up. Then they passed a Schraffts and she said her feet were freezing and a cup of hot chocolate would help.

This Terry drank cup after cup of coffee, talking nonstop. Siri was so bored she started reading the flavors of ice cream and the different soda drinks. Then she scanned the cozy room for someone else she'd rather be with, but Schraffts was full of old ladies and children, and even that crowd thinned as dusk approached.

"Sociology, huh?" he said, when she was sure he had forgotten. "That's the study of society, of people in groups. Gemeinschaft and Gesellschaft. They can't decide, though, whether they're do-gooders or scientists. I've read a little."

Sociology was a twentieth-century discipline, and really just an offshoot of history, political science and blahblah-blah. Finally, it was dark enough for the Christmas lights to come on, so back out they walked.

In the dark, Siri liked him a little better. He took off his glove to hold her hand, although she left hers on. For two blocks they just looked ahead to where the park lights burned in the frigid air. "Where's New Federal?" he said, suddenly.

"In Connecticut."

"Small town, small city, suburb?" he asked.

"It's small," Siri said, wondering if he were going to start up again.

He laughed. "You don't waste any words. I've never met a teenaged girl I couldn't get to talk. Most girls like to."

So—to stop him from rattling on about girls and what he knew about them—Siri told him things about Esther. But he seized upon everything, sometimes even before she had it all out. If Esther's father ran a hospital laundry in Waltham, she must be on scholarship, right? Well, why couldn't she do better than St. Mary's? They must be devout Catholics if the brother went into the priesthood in high school, so that must be why she went there. Okay, what else?

Siri felt the strain of another interrogation. "Why do you want to know?" she said.

"I don't really. It's just something to talk about. Are you friends or just sharing a room? Doesn't sound like you have a whole lot in common."

We don't, Siri almost said, but in a instant, she could see where that might lead. The roommates didn't have much in common—maybe nothing at all—and that meant she was dumb and Esther smart; Esther was interesting and she——. At any rate, all this jabbering was the opposite of interesting and Esther would agree, so there.

So Siri told him Esther's idea—"theory," she called it—about jotting down the first words of the first lecture of every class, or the first words out of people's mouths which, incidentally, would be useless in his case because those words were lost now. He had said so much and about so many different things that she wouldn't in a million years remember. And Esther might well ask her. Whatever they were, those first words, they were gone forever.

Sure enough, he was stunned into silence, then spent the next fifteen minutes, or as long as it took to find the car, "wracking his brains," as he said, to find which of perhaps twenty different things he might have said that day when he picked her up. He had a photographic but not "aural" memory, but now he really did want to remember and, thanks, it was the most interesting thing anyone had said all week. He'd try it out; he could foresee what the "payoff" might be. Especially for someone going into medicine, or the foreign service. Just thinking about it made him lean toward medicine. At least for the moment.

Siri was elated, a new sensation. He wouldn't stop complimenting her, or thanking her. He might even write a short paper; better still, a newspaper column.

But, as Siri was thinking, lying awake, waiting for Esther's breathing to shift, and to blow out the snag, *this* was not her idea, although she had gotten the credit and the phone call every night the past week until finally Phone Duty didn't even bother to knock on their door. It was Esther's. Siri's new idea, built upon Esther's old one, was something she'd learned that night with Terry. She didn't yet have the words or even a picture to describe it, and it was keeping her awake. Ideas were free, but they were worth something to people. Collecting them was as easy as staying awake. The hard part was figuring out what people didn't know that they could use, and would value. According to Esther, books were full of ideas, but Siri knew that these were never in a useful form. The best ideas came directly from people—even Teddy had some, but Esther was a gold mine, and didn't even know it. Now that Esther's breathing had cleared the obstruction, Siri could think without the irritation. Why didn't Esther know the value of her ideas? She knew everything else.

By morning, Esther had a cold from the crying, but she was going to class anyway. Once she was dressed and gone—and no chance of her flying back for a pen or text-book (first-period bells had rung; the corridor was still)— Siri opened the drawer to Esther's desk. Esther was a slob—papers, gum wrappers, slide rule, Mass cards, letters from Mr. Ferry, drafts of papers; she even had a half-filled book of Green Stamps (why?). But Siri found what she was looking for: Esther's daybook—a diary, really, but Esther called it a daybook. Siri had seen it before and even opened it, but because Sybele was such a snoop, Dad had said: don't pry into other people's affairs; you might think you want to know what they're thinking, but, believe me, you don't. This sounded stupid to Siri, stupid, unnecessary and irrelevant, but she did remember it and put Esther's daybook back where she found it. In no way did she want to be like Sybele. And Dad was right: she didn't want to know. Esther said what she thought; you didn't have to pry things out of her.

But now, Siri thought there might be more. If it took three months to hear about Danny the priest and that was such a big deal, what else was there? Siri had the idea there and then, at ten after nine, of buying herself a daybook and copying down what she found in Esther's. The thought made her head buzz.

Esther had made four long entries. They were all labeled "weekend," which was odd because Siri had never seen her writing in the daybook and they spent most of the weekends together, except for the afternoon date with Terry and a Sunday visit from the Ferrys when Siri was invited to "eat out," as they called it, but said no because Esther had warned that they'd end up, as always, at Lum's, eating wurst and kraut. Siri had never had kraut, and wasn't tempted by the sound of it.

At the back of the daybook, she found a title, "Principal Flaws," and a columns of words. Some of the words were written slanted forwards, some backwards. Occasionally, a word was block-printed.

Awkward, bashful, depressed, deceitful, fat, fool, grandiose, hefty, immature, jaded, (Siri jumped ahead), wimpy, wasteful, yellow-belly, zits.

There was another title, "Prime Qualities," and a short column: smart, healthy, self-controlled. Honest was crossed out.

Siri had the urge to add a few words of her own. For one thing, Esther didn't really know what she was like. Siri's list would come closer. She was bored, though, with the idea of thinking that hard about Esther. So she flipped back to the middle where she found quotes from other people. "The world is all there is that is the case." She didn't see why something like this was valuable. "Our treasure is where our beehives of knowledge stand. We are forever under-way toward them, as born winged-animals and honey-gath-erers of the spirit." Half of them sounded crazy ("After great pain, a formal feeling comes"), and the other half des-perate. Maybe it was because they were talking to Esther and she brought this out in them. This got Siri thinking, but since she was still reading, she jotted down the idea in pen-cil so she wouldn't forget, but also so she could erase it before Esther got back from class. "It's you," she wrote, "who's making them say these things. They'd never say this to me."

On another page was a list of books. *Madame Bovary* was there with an X2. Other things Esther must have read in the library because Siri had never seen the books lying around the room. In a page somewhere in the middle and sur-rounded by big margins was Esther's name, written in dif-ferent handwritings with "Miss," "Doctor," "The Honorable Lady," and—unbelievable!—"Pres. Esther T. Ferry." Was she crazy! Siri crossed it out.

It was almost time for second period and there was less danger of catching a cold, so Siri dressed. (She wasn't showering because of the dry-skin condition, just slapping on baby oil and splashing her face with water.) She looked at herself in the bathroom mirror: dead tired with rings under her eyes and yellowish skin. And the face was bone-thin; her chin came to a point and her neck was lost in the thick cowl collar. Esther loved using the word "intellectual," usually as a term to describe what St. M.'s students were not. But intellectual was what Siri was becoming. Now she was certain, having read the boners in Esther's daybook, that she, Siri, was the real intellectual. For one, she was looking the part, and she felt it, too. What did it feel like? Well—Siri whispered to the image in the mirror—you were always hungry, starving sometimes (like now), but food (at least the slop in the caf) wasn't right, or enough, or it was too much. Second, your eyesight grew weaker through the strain of being awake half the night, thinking, with your eyes wide open; third, things happening on the outside mattered less and less. What really mattered was what was inside. Inside was where the thinking happened. It wasn't feeling. Feeling was never too important in Siri's mind. Dad, for instance, didn't feel anything and he was fine. Sybele felt every little thing and seemed like a fool. Esther liked to cry, but Siri never cried. Was feeling good for anything? Siri shut her eyes tight. When she opened them, there in the mirror with her own blurry face was someone's else's. Siri shut her eyes.

"I heard talking in here," someone else—a nun!—said.

Siri shut her eyes again.

"Are you quite all right?"

"I'm fine," said Siri, finding her voice and an easy out: "I was memorizing a poem."

"Why aren't you in class?"

"I'm going to class. I'm on my way right now."

"Is that the proper way to speak to a religious? Open your eyes."

Siri opened them. She was right in thinking this was not one of the regular nuns. This one was all in white. Was she even in the same order?

"I didn't go to Catholic school," Siri said.

"You're attending a Catholic college. Shouldn't you know better?"

The nun had an accent which Siri couldn't place. St. Mary's nuns were from Ireland. That's what Esther said, so it could be that.

"I'm going to be late, Sister," she said.

"Tell me your name."

"Esther Ferry," said Siri, without hesitating.

"Well, you run along then. I won't detain you."

Who was she, Siri was thinking, padding back to the room to find her flats, to push people around that way? Nuns—even more than priests—thought they had this prerogative. It was why Siri hated being around them.

At lunch, when the shattering din was beaten down by a bell-ringing nun, the introduction was made, and a special welcome asked for the Reverend Mother General, visiting from the mother house in Calgary. (It was the same one).

"I met her in the bathroom," Siri said to Esther, as soon as the din built up again.

Esther laughed. "That's what you get for bunking classes. What was she doing in there?"

Mother Domitia would be on campus for a week. She would have conferences with students who suspected (or hoped) that they might have a special calling. All students should look into their hearts, the dean said, with this unique opportunity at hand. "Why don't you go?" Siri said to Esther. "They could use an atheist for a change." Esther laughed, but then received a personal note from Mother Domitia with a conference time, and decided to go anyway: imagine what this opener would be like! (I wonder how she knew my name, she said to Siri.)

Hard though she tried, Siri couldn't get used to going every single day to her classes. In high school, it was all in one building and you could relax in the room and wait for each teacher to show up, all frazzled and rushed. If you were there, you were there for the day. It was tedious, but took no effort. This finding your way by yourself and every hour having to fight a crowd out of one classroom only to fight a crowd to get into another one that might not even be in the same building, and having to keep straight all the room numbers and subjects and the books that went with them, was well nigh impossible.

Esther tried to help. She wrote out a schedule with a map; they even did a dry run late one afternoon. Siri could get started—especially since Esther sometimes walked her to class. She might arrive on time for theology and sit through that, even though it was a warm room and a hissing, spitting radiator. She even took notes—not always in the same place, but she had them in the binder somewhere. That teacher, whose name Siri could never remember, and who practically faded into the wall—she was so plain and always wore the same suit—was supposed to be talking about the Bible but was always going off on a tangent. Plus, her voice was hard to listen to: hoarse with a smoker's cough, always clearing her throat, and every time she cleared it, Siri would lose the beginning of the sentence. The Old Testament, or OT, as the teacher called it, was not, in Siri's mind, a significant part of the Bible. Siri was waiting for her to get around to the NT, something she knew about from sermons and religion classes. When Siri mentioned this to a girl on their corridor was when she discovered that they were *never* getting there. Her part was saved for another course. This stupid class was only the OT, so waiting was a mistake. How to catch up was the problem, even with the notes she'd borrowed, because the Bible stories—after Adam and Eve—were boring, and some were unbelievable to anyone but a child.

The next class, on health, was in the basement of the student union. It was a science requirement. Health was a dumb subject and could be skipped because the human body was something Siri knew inside out. Then it turned out that the subject wasn't really health—or about keeping healthy. The teacher—a man, one of the few—was turning health and the human body into chemistry, which was Greek to Siri. Read the textbook, Esther had said, and Siri had tried, but right away the subject turned into equations, using letters for chemicals. Even when she looked up the answers in the back of the book (where Esther said they'd be), it didn't make the problems any clearer. Seeing these equations with their arrows, equal signs, numbers and blanks filled Siri with rage. And after these formulas, there were molecules to come! Copying out these equations, as Esther had advised, did not help. Watching Esther solve them convinced Siri that this was something she would never get. The symbols were confusing and the numbers were crazy. Each chemical had a number, but sometimes the number changed. H_2O was the easiest to remember because it was water, and Siri had memorized it in high school. But O had a number and H_2O didn't tell you what that number was. This was cause for tears, but Siri wasn't going to cry over anything as stupid as this.

The next class, right before lunch with everybody's stomach growling, and Siri nearly dead from exhaustion, was history, where at least she could sit next to Esther—if Esther didn't get there too early and parade to the front row. Siri liked history because all the freshmen took it and the class was large. Sitting in the back row, you could doodle or close your eyes if it got too hot. Mr. Whitman had too much to say to bother calling on students for their opinions; and if he did call on anyone, it was usually Esther.

Esther—unlike even the smartest and most eager-beaver freshman—was always caught up with the reading. She used Siri's books. Esther spent so much time with Siri's books that they smelled of Dial soap. Even the pictures in these books were dull, but Siri was reading one of them and making her own underlines. She was many chapters behind, but she understood what she was reading and could even remember some of it: Babylonia, Assyria, Mesopotamia, Hannibal on his elephant and Cyrus the Great. She was getting to the point in time (o) where history (B.C.) became theology (A.D.), and that part she knew—catacombs, gladiators and martyrs crucified upside down. When she wasn't dead tired, or in a bad mood, she listened to Mr. Whitman, who was now talking about Charlemagne, and all you had to do was move your finger up the ancient map to Gaul, which Siri knew was France. In this way, things were coming together. It wasn't easy, but if she had coffee with dinner and took a couple of NoDoz, and they kept the overhead light on and the window open and Phone Duty wasn't running in and out, she could read five to ten pages, read them again (which Esther recommended), and then scan the underlines; and that stretch of history was straightened out. She'd never catch up, no matter what Esther said, she'd never be a genius, but she was starting to know things.

Esther, meanwhile, had fallen in love with Mr. Whitman. Siri knew because she read about it in the daybook. At first, Mr. Whitman's words were in there with everyone else's. But little by little, fewer people were quoted and soon (yesterday or the day before), the entries were all him. Siri knew because she had heard him say these same things about medieval France and troubadour poetry.

The day after Esther had her conference with Mother Domitia ("she kept looking at me like she knew me, but I'd never met her before"), and was invited back (faculty liked talking to Esther and treated her like an equal, which made some girls resent Esther), she went to Mr. Whitman's Wednesday office hour.

That was nothing new. She often went and spent fifteen minutes going over the extra-credit essay question. This time, instead of going for fifteen minutes at the top of the hour, so they could watch *General Hospital,* she was gone for the whole hour.

Siri was watching a rerun of *Dobie Gillis* when Esther walked into the lounge. "I'm going to take a shower," she said. "I'll see you in the dining hall."

But Siri followed her out. "Why?" she said to Esther's back. "Why, in the middle of the afternoon, are you going to take a shower? Answer me!" she said, and still the girl didn't turn around. Siri ran ahead and stopped her. "Your face is all red," she said.

"I'm sweating," Esther said. "That's why I'm taking a shower. Wait for me."

Siri flopped on the bed to unfold this mystery. She was ready to pounce when Esther reentered with streaming hair, making drippy footprints on the wooden floor. "Where've you been?"

"I'll tell you later."

"Tell me now."

"Let's eat, then I'll tell you. I don't want the others to hear."

"To hear what?"

"Wait," Esther said, pulling a sweater over her head.

"Aren't you going to dry your hair?"

"Nope."

"Tell me now," Siri said. "No one's listening."

"Let's go," Esther said. "I'm ready. I'll tell you after."

And, after all the buildup, there was no story to tell. Mr. Whitman had lent Esther a book was all, a French paperback with yellow covers and tiny print. It was an old, tattered book, but Esther carried it with her everywhere. It smelled a little of pipe smoke and sometimes Esther fell asleep with the book open over her face. At first, Esther didn't want Siri to touch it, but then Siri reminded her that all of her own books, bought for classes, were on Esther's bookshelf, or on Esther's desk, so was it fair that this special book be off-limits? Even after Esther pointed out that it was in French and Siri couldn't understand it, she still wanted to spend time with it.

Esther gave in, and it wasn't pipe smoke it smelled of; it was mold, Siri insisted, sniffing it so hard she got dust up her nose and then sneezed on the book, making a wet patch impossible to smooth out.

The book was called *The Second Sex,* Esther said, and the title—almost the same in French—said as much. Siri was shocked until Esther explained—then proved by translating a paragraph—that it wasn't about "doing it"; it was about men as the first sex and women as the second. It was a book of radical philosophy, Mr. Whitman said, that students in a Catholic, all girls college, where just wearing pants on campus required a covering raincoat, should read.

Siri was certain that women were second only in France, but Esther said, what about your own mother? which made Siri think.

"What about her?"

"She's a wreck."

"That's because she has a screw loose," said Siri, mimicking Esther.

"That's true, but she's also stuck in the house, miserable

and depressed. Did she ever work in her life? Did she go to college?"

"She went here!" Siri said.

"Yeah, well," Esther replied, "enough said, right?"

"*We* go here, don't forget," Siri said.

Esther wanted Siri to read the book, but not this copy. First, they had to find it in English. Meanwhile, Esther continued to cherish the musty paperback. Siri even caught her licking the title on the cover.

That Mr. Whitman was engaged was a major problem, as far as Siri could see. This was one of the first tidbits Esther pried out of the reticent historian. Esther insisted this was not at all a problem. She had no romantic interest in an intellectual twice their age.

"Don't make me laugh," said Siri.

"I'm telling you the truth as I see it."

"Then you're blind."

That was only part of it. The reason Esther was blind was that she'd never had a real boyfriend. (Neither had Siri, because the more she thought about it, Christo didn't count; he couldn't even kiss right.)

She was in love, face it. (Siri couldn't admit that her certainty was based on reading the entries in a private diary.)

No, she wasn't in love, Esther said, but Mr. Whitman was an education in himself. Every word out of his mouth was a gem, worth writing down.

No kidding, Siri wanted to say.

And now he was starting to give her books outside of class. Even Esther's French wasn't good enough to read the thick book, although she spent hours flipping through it with a dictionary open. It was Siri who had the bright idea of seeing if the library had the book in English. It didn't, but it could be found in the interlibrary circuit of Catholic schools St. M's belonged to, and—although there were restrictions on this volume—Siri, revealing the extent of her family's generosity to the college, managed to get it within a week.

Siri read the English while Esther was pretending to read the French. What a farce! After a while, they traded. Siri dozed while Esther read the English, first aloud, then to herself.

Mr. Whitman, who Siri admitted was cute in a dusty kind of way, was giving a public lecture right before Christmas vacation. Esther introduced him. The lecture was on career opportunities. In it, he told a straggly group of about twenty freshmen that young women should think beyond early education and marriage as their goal. The world was opening up for women, although here they may not be aware of it. It was possible, he said, for girls like themselves from average homes and so-so high schools to get a real education, if they worked at it, if they selected their courses carefully, if they pursued travel abroad whether or not the school sponsored it, if they exploited the resources of the city of Boston. If they read, if they kept their minds open, and were skeptical, the effort, he said, would pay off.

After the lecture, Esther followed Mr. Whitman, with two other girls from history class, to the coffee shop. Siri watched from a distance. Esther sat right next to the professor and kept her eyes fastened upon his face.

Little by little, the roommates learned more about Mr. Whitman—Esther from the horse's mouth and Siri from the daybook, or immediately after his office hours when Esther couldn't hold it in. He was engaged, but his girl-friend was in France. He lived with his mother on Beacon Hill. (Esther explained where Beacon Hill was and what it meant to live there.) He wrote poetry and had a poem published in a special kind of magazine for writers. He'd had rheumatic fever as a kid, which is when he started reading history.

Siri wanted to hear more about the girlfriend. Was she French or just in France for a visit? In any case, she must be beautiful.

She wasn't, Esther said. She'd been in a car accident as a kid and had an artificial eye. He's available, Siri concluded, and even said.

Siri noticed one thing. Esther wasn't crying in the night anymore, and it wasn't because the loser of an ex-priest brother had straightened out. He'd left the nurse and two kids and was working with prisoners and living in the slum part of Waltham. Mrs. Ferry had had a nervous breakdown over it, but in their family, all that meant was the grand-mother moved in to cook the meals and do the housework. Mrs. Ferry was "sedated," as Esther put it, and that meant something stronger than the Valium Sybele took on bad days. Then, one of the brother's kids pulled down a pot of boiling coffee over his head and was in the hospital for over a week. Even though Esther was on the phone with her father and sister-in-law, who were all "worried sick," Esther slept through the night, lost a little weight (she needed to) and looked better than ever.

Esther and Siri were both dreading Christmas and the vacation. First of all, it wasn't a real vacation if all it meant was three weeks spent at home, and they had to come back to exams in January. Then, Mr. Whitman, whom Siri was warming up to—he'd had both girls to tea in his office, and he read them his poem from *Poets of Boston,* and told them about his research and where it was leading him—was going to France to visit Beverly. He'd send them each a postcard if he remembered. Siri noted her address and Esther's, then crossed hers out and wrote the school post-office number. "I'm coming back early," she explained, and caught Esther's popped eyes. Then Esther crossed out her address and wrote her post-office number.

"Can you come back early and stay here?" the teacher asked.

Esther looked at Siri. "The nuns are here all the time."

"So they are."

Mr. Whitman would return just after New Year's and if they managed to come back early, maybe they'd like to come into Boston and meet his mother, have a cup of tea, and maybe visit the MFA or catch a rehearsal of the BSO, depending on the day.

And it was all very cozy, like that, which made Mr. Whitman seem much less romantic, even to Esther—or so she said.

When Dad drove up in a new car (rebuilt blue MG) to pick her up, Siri was sorry to leave. Esther had talked all morning about ways to make the time go fast, but also be "productive." The textbooks were going home with Siri, as were Esther's history notes. If Siri could afford one failure—and that was a big if—she had to narrow it down by catching up in all her other courses. Esther was going to concentrate on *The Second Sex*. She was taking the English version. Siri was tired of it anyway. It was hard and tedious reading and it got you nowhere. She could never remember anything from it.

With *Madame Bovary* it was different. She loved that book and was taking it home to read it again. Once she figured out who it was really about—Sybele (and here *The Second Sex* had helped her)—it was easier to swallow what happened, and the dread went away. She became eager to see stupid, stubborn Emma, who didn't know what she had when she had it, bite the dust. Once Emma took the poison, though, and wasn't saved at the last minute by the druggist or the Paris doctors (which Siri was sure would happen), she changed her mind. It wasn't about Sybele, or anyone she knew, although there was some resemblance to Irene. Esther complimented her, upon hearing this: now she was able to use literature to understand life in the abstract, which was the whole idea of it. "Wait'll Dad sees me reading this!" Siri said, as she packed the paperback with the piles of textbooks, which she knew in her heart she'd never open.

When Siri and Dad got home—they'd driven with the top down on this unseasonably mild December day, so although there was no talk, Dad reached over to squeeze

Siri's hand and yelled over the deafening wind that his little girl seemed awfully skinny, but before she got to yell back, he was back into his Benny Goodman tape—she discovered she'd packed Esther's new daybook by mistake. It was tucked inside the cover of the health binder where Siri had shoved it when Esther came back from the shower earlier than expected. Sybele was helping her unpack—and Siri let her do it—talking the whole time about things that had happened at home. (Who cared!) And also, which of the things needed washing, dry cleaning or were too "shot" to be sent back to college. Siri, she said several times, seemed to have gotten a lot of wear out of her clothes, especially the cashmere sweaters. (Siri could have explained that three or four girls had worn those sweaters, one nearly every day, because everyone liked them.)

She thought her room looked the same—smaller, yes, but just as girly-girl, as Esther would say, with the canopied bed her mother was sitting on, and the frilled skirt on the antique vanity. Everything was squeaky clean—mirrors, floor, windows even, where the sun came pouring in. Siri and Esther kept their shades pulled, even in daytime. "I like artificial light," Esther was forever saying. What's artificial about it? Siri must have asked her a hundred times and still didn't get it, but smiled now to think (carumba!) it meant light that was not the sun!

Siri pulled the blind cord, but the slatted light was almost as glary. There was no place to sit in this babyish room; there was no real desk, and how could you read in bed if the lamp was that far away from the pillow? And it didn't even have a lightbulb!

"What's wrong?" her mother was saying. "You've got a terrible puss on."

Siri had never liked the all-white room. It had been Sybele's idea to buy the canopied bed and then pile it up with pillows of all different sizes. The bed was too little, yet it took up too much space. She searched through the book-bag Esther had lent her (cloth with a cord tie) for *Bovary,* and left her mother to finish with the clothes. She decided then and there to sleep in the spare room.

No one was in the den, which tended to be dark, so Siri switched on a floor lamp and sat in the leather chair her father had broken in. It smelled like him and that was nice. She opened the book, and here was Teddy.

But Teddy, an only child for three months now and sus-picious of this skinny, weird-looking sister with yellow stains on the fingers that held the book, didn't begin the spiel that Siri expected. "You readin'?" he said.

"What's it look like?"

Teddy plunked himself down on the chintz settee their mother had had moved into the den when Dad started spending his free time in there. The doctor had said no more birds or he'd be too crippled to hold up a fork, so Dad, Teddy explained to Siri, when she spotted the flower couch, went back to his stamp collection and his bird watching, and moved all his things in here. Mom didn't want to watch TV alone, so she took her needlepoint into the den. Teddy had the TV room to himself and he and Christo (they were best friends) played chess and watched old movies. Christo spent more time at the Sorensons' than he did at home.

This was all tiresome to hear. If anything, home life was worse than she remembered it. So much had happened to Siri, but nothing had happened to them—and they didn't even seem to know it. Even Teddy was satisfied with two or three dumb questions, before opening up his *Mad*.

Realizing she needed to talk to someone, now that there was no Esther, Siri got up, grabbed the *Mad* and sat on it. "You came in here," she said to her brother, "so talk to me."

Teddy wanted to know if she had a new boyfriend.

"Are you going to blab to Christo, if I tell you?"

Teddy thought. Then he blurted it out: "Christo has a new girlfriend, Sear. He wanted me to tell you if I saw you before he did."

Siri looked at her little brother. He was immature. He'd always be immature. He'd never catch up with her, especially now that she was in college. Siri felt her face burning and now her eyes were stinging. A thousand sleepless nights—or so it seemed—had eaten away at all her self-control (and, according to Esther, she didn't have much to start with). Pretty soon, she was crying, crying so hard that Teddy went to find his mother, but on the way, ran into his father. When Teddy opened the door to the den, with his mother right behind him, they saw Dad in his chair with Siri on his lap, rocking her, even though the leather chair was not a rocker.

"My baby sweetheart," he was saying, and the sound of it made Teddy feel like crying, too.

"What? What is it?" his mother was asking in that shrill voice that scared him.

"Shut up," Siri said. "Go away."

And before long, they were all worked up and even Teddy was yelling at his dad, who never rocked him in his lap, and mother, too, saying how Dad was allergic to her, or so he seemed.

And Siri saying how she hated this family and was happy to be away, rolling off Dad's lap, stalking to her door, slamming it, locking it.

Which was how the long letter (now five or six pages long, and written on both sides) got started to Esther, written on pages of Esther's new daybook.

Christmas wasn't much better. Dad bought Sybele a string of pearls that reminded him, he told Siri coming back from the jewelry store, of what Sybele was like in college with her black sweaters and skirts and pearl studs. But the string Dad bought was too tight around her neck, and too youthful anyway. Sybele liked more coverage around her throat where the soft skin puckered a little, as Siri was kind enough to point out. She planned to exchange the pearls for gold hoops, an idea that Dad didn't care for. Siri wanted them to keep the string and give it to her, but she already had pearls and don't be always thinking of yourself, her mother said—a remark which started that day's war, which spilled onto Christmas dinner at Aunt Bay's, when a still-seething Siri stomped all over her mother's attempt to tell the story of homecoming weekend at Harvard, when she was pinned by Dad, by saying that at least her generation—hers and Esther's—was going to college for more than just getting a husband.

Siri said this at dessert, as Aunt Bay was lighting the fig pudding, and Sybele pouring coffee from the Sorenson silver service. Her hands were shaking, as they always did—and Siri watched for it—when contact with the vintage silver pots reminded her mother of what Dad's younger sister had gotten that, by rights, should have gone to the wife of the eldest son. She nearly dropped the pot, spilling staining liquid on the linen tablecloth.

"Watch your mouth, child," Uncle Dukie said, but Dad defended Siri. It was clear, he said, that a college education for girls wasn't going to waste. But, he turned to Siri, if they weren't there to trap a man, what were they doing?

But Siri wasn't performing for this company, and said so.

"Look at you," Sybele said, sipping her coffee, after dosing it with liqueur. "You're not even twenty years old. What do you know about life?"

"A hell of a lot more than you ever did," Siri snarled.

"Leave the table," Uncle Duke said, standing. "Leave the table this minute. We don't have talk like this at Christmas."

"Excuse me, Derek," Dad said in a small voice.

"I'm going," said Siri, standing up so fast her chair fell backwards.

"I love you, Dad," Siri said, circling the table to kiss his pate.

This "scene" was going into the letter. Who else but Esther would understand? Also going in was the fact that Siri had gotten nothing but useless garbage for Christmas—clothes that didn't fit ("how," her mother had said, "was I to know you'd lost so much weight, you now wear a child's size?"), records she didn't want (who listened to Peter, Paul & Mary or the Kingston Trio, much less the soundtrack to *The Sound of Music*?). She did receive a portable electric typewriter that'd come in handy, since Esther didn't even have a manual, and gift certificates. And tons of unperfumed soap and lotion, now that the dermatologist had outlawed anything with detergent, disinfectant or scent, and advised two oatmeal baths a week, when she had the use of a tub, and the excision of all irritating tags and labels. No wool, no synthetics. "If you're not careful," Dr. Motta had said, "you'll end up in a leper colony." Siri laughed, and luckily Sybele was out feeding the parking meter.

Dr. Motta thought the dryness might be stress related, so he prescribed a mild tranquilizer to relax her at night. The sleep problems he referred to the pediatrician, but Siri had had enough of doctors, and she didn't need much sleep anymore: she felt fine. At lunch that day, in Bonwit's tearoom, she took one of her mother's Chesterfields, lit it, choked and stubbed it out in the cream cheese of her date-bread sandwich, practically untouched—then apologized. She would put her mother, she wrote to Esther, in the nut house before long, if she wasn't careful. Not a good thing, she added, because someone would have to come back from college to look after Dad and Teddy.

Siri was wrong about the family. Something had changed in the months she'd been away. Immature as he was and would always be, Teddy (or Ted, as he now liked to be called) wasn't underfoot as much. He had schoolfriends, and Christo, whom Siri was avoiding. Sybele, with no daughter to pester and tease, had started a bridge club and swam at the Y. She was taking classes in cordon-bleu cooking school in Hartford. Dad had his own hobbies: he was developing film and printing pictures in the basement; he was taking flying lessons and had donated his woodshop to the vocational high school. That "the family," as Sybele called the three of them, spent time together in Dad's den, which Sybele called "the study," was in itself a miracle. Siri didn't care to join them, and her absence drew Teddy away to play table hockey.

"What are you up to?" Siri asked Esther, day after Christmas, the first time she thought to call her. Writing the long letter was one thing, but calling Esther and trying to be the person who used to live in 403 Great Hall, with the shades pulled all day long and Madame Bovary and Mr. Whitman, was more than Siri could manage. Hearing Esther's voice, she almost screamed.

But, surprisingly, it took less than a minute to fall into the familiar ways.

"Hey, Room!" Esther said.

"What are you up to? What'dya get for Christmas?" Siri asked. "No, don't tell me."

That made Esther laugh. Then came the list: gold-leaf, red leather St. Joseph's daily missal, "top of the line," a couple of nighties and a bath kit.

Siri waited, but the list was finished. "That's nice," she said.

"What's nice about it?" (And didn't that sound like Esther.)

"I was just being polite."

"Don't bother," Esther said. "It's not your style."

"I'm writing you a long letter."

"You are?"

But, by the time Siri sent the letter, and all her clothes had been altered, it was almost time to come back to campus. Vacation was over and exams just around the corner. How much studying was Siri getting done at home, where there were no distractions? Not much, she thought, catching sight of the bookbag; but none was closer to it.

It turned out Dad wasn't the least interested in *Bovary* (he'd heard of it, but it was a woman's novel, wasn't it?). No, it wasn't, Siri informed him, wracking her brain to recall what Esther had said about the author—he was a man!—that would impress someone like Dad, who liked books about airplanes and dogs. Sybele said she thought she might have read the book herself at St. M's. "No, you did not!" Siri was quick to say because Sybele was still a person who tried to draw attention to herself. "This is a private conversation," Siri added.

"Well, I'm here, too," her mother replied.

"I was talking to Dad," Siri said.

"I noticed the novel right away when you came home," Sybele went on (as if anyone cared!). "I did more reading than you in college. I was an English major."

"*I was an English major,*" Siri said, mimicking her mother's piping tone, a few notches higher.

"What's your major going to be, Siri Susan?" Dad asked,

interrupting what was a mere shadow of the cat fights he was always expected to break up. And it wasn't because Siri was more mature: she wasn't, but she was not the same girl they had sent to college in September. She was wasting!

"Math," Siri said, "or history. Math or history, one or the other."

Sybele was chuckling to herself and Siri ready to blast her, when the phone rang, and Siri darted for it.

But Teddy already had it: it was for him and he held his sister off with one arm. It wasn't hard: she was the "hundred-pound weakling" that he and Chris laughed about in the back of the comics.

It wasn't so funny, though, when Siri bit his hand. And so hard that it broke the skin. Teddy dropped the phone, swearing (this was a new one). Sybele saw the teeth marks—like a rat's or a bear cub's—and was set to slap the awful child hard, but the child was already (door slammed) barricaded in her bedroom.

Donald must get involved, and he did, cleaning Teddy's double puncture wound and dressing it and taking the boy out to the photo shop, but really to the Oysterman's, where they could watch a game and Dad could have a few. ("You can't take that child to a bar!" Sybele said. "I might need you here," she added, but Donald and Ted, as Daddy called Teddy, were halfway out the door. Daddy was teaching Ted how to play nine-ball, although not today, when the injured hand should rest. "I'm fine, Dad," Sybele heard, as the front door closed. "When are you coming back?" Sybele shouted to the closed car, as it rolled down the driveway.)

"You're a hateful girl," Sybele didn't even have to say through the keyhole, because Siri knew what everyone thought of her that Saturday. And it was no different from what they had always thought. Sybele didn't like to use the word "bad" when speaking about her own family, but she now recognized what the sisters had insinuated, but were too hypocritical to say. What they would say—if the Sorenson family hadn't paid for the Lady altar and made an annual gift for altar flowers—was that "Sara," as they insisted on slurring the vowels in a name that, to their knowledge, derived from no known saint, was bad at the core, that she would be a "trial," a "hardship" for the family. They didn't dare say, as had a Girl Scout leader, that someone else bore responsibility—not for the meanness; that was innate—but for the girl's horridness. "And who would that be?" Sybele wished she had asked.

Sybele stood outside her daughter's bedroom door and listened—not a sound. Sudden footsteps made her jump, though, and she fled downstairs to make the first cup of tea in that endless, dreary day. Did she fear for her own skin? she wondered, sitting at the kitchen table and examining the backs of her smooth, unaged hands. Then she pulled her sweater to the knuckles. Siri had to be gotten back to that college before anything else happened. And there could be no question of a transfer to New Federal junior college, as the dean had suggested in a note that came in Friday's mail. St. M's had admitted her and now—Sybele steamed her face over the tea—she was their responsibility. "I can't control her," she would say, if it came to that.

Because Siri had bitten her brother, and had the taste of

his skin (yick) in her mouth, and there was nothing in the bedroom to rinse it out (she looked in the mirror to see if any flecks of skin were on her teeth, gagging at the thought), she now detested him more than the others. She hated them all, and there was more hate than they could absorb: Sybele and Teddy, so a little slopped onto Dad, a first, but Dad had married Sybele and Teddy was his child. Siri thought of jumping out the window—she opened it: first the inside window, then the storm, but the air was so cold and had that wintry rawness that cut into the skin and took your breath away, so she closed it, but the storm window stuck in its metal grooves, and she had just enough energy to squeeze down the inside window, dropping to the floor and rolling up into a shivering, sweaty ball. But the extra hate was still outflowing and it would catch up with someone else if she didn't keep ahead of it. She pulled open her dresser drawers, and then the closet doors, yanking out piles of sweaters and dresses on hangers, skirts, scarves, hats, underwear, until the floor was thick with wool, silk and cotton, a crazy soup of solid and striped and printed. She sat in the middle and wailed.

Sunday, the last day at home, Sybele helped Siri pack (after the clothing flood was sopped up, the sight of which might have ignited another battle if Sybele hadn't been too tired and a little hungover, and still medicated from yesterday's anguish, to react to the mess that only a she-devil could make of the gifts of a loving mother and father). But she cried when the girl set off with her father in the family station wagon. (Sybele offered to take her, but Donald said they needed time together, father and daughter. He was acting—this was typical—as if this were Sybele's fault.) Siri closed the front door (Dad had both hands full of luggage) without a backward glance. She was never coming back to this dump.

Donald—for now he was Donald to his daughter—drove in silence until the last landmark of New Federal fell behind and the large, smooth-running vehicle was rolling on the freeway. He liked to drive and it didn't matter whom he had with him. Driving created fullness and tranquility, a state he was capable of inducing from the poorest materials (Sybele, the children, meal times, client conferences), but was a natural effluent of mechanic routines (driving, mowing, shoveling snow), not to mention the superplus to be found in the ecstasy of carving wood and filling in boxes of his bird log, framing billiard balls, contemplating a chessboard without the distractions of an ongoing game. Driving was bliss and Donald did a lot of it, assigning to himself all the family errands, which he spun out in separate units and always took the long way. He drove fast and cracked all the windows, winter and summer, so that even if he had company, their voices were lost in the slurry of wind, whirr and whistle, with radio or tapes if necessary. He stockpiled these hours of mechanical routine to spread like fertilizer over the rough spots of daily life.

But he liked his daughter, Siri Susan, as he liked to call her, who turned out to be a chip off nobody's block. So far, she'd been an unrewarding child, girl, daughter, student and family member—he could see her shortcomings; he was not blind. As a social entity, she was a minus, but as a presence, she was ideal: silent, unintrusive (unless she were fighting with her mother), snide and funny as hell, when and if she opened her mouth. He didn't understand the problem she created for others. He assumed they were all fools. Most people were.

Did he love Siri Susan? He knew he did and a lot more than he loved the son or the wife. In spite of what people thought, you couldn't control or program feelings, but you could keep them to yourself. Feeling was fuel, like driving or mowing the grass; it was an energy, or drug, if you liked, that could be used then or stored. No one knew what produced it, where it came from, or where it really wanted to go. Feeling was raw wood that must not be worked until it was treated, dried and seasoned. That way, life could be contained in a single human skin, without the contamination of others.

Thus, Donald was busy with his thoughts. Siri was thinking, too. All this time at home had been wasted. She was worn out, thinner and drier (even with her mother's lotions and oils, and the doctor's prescription creams), but nothing had happened. Maybe something had been lost. Her mind seemed heavy and sluggish. It was painful to think. Facts were sharp as tacks. What were they? She hated her family and they hated her. She didn't know it until now, sitting next to Dad, that lunkhead. She hated being alive, but death was not an easy out, as it had been for Emma. When Emma did it, she had nothing going for her. It was easy and the poison was available. People around her were ready for her to do it. The stage was set and Emma was on it. Compared to that, Siri's situation was pathetic. She hadn't even lived yet.

"Shut up, Donald," she felt like saying, because Dad was talking and audible, which was unusual. He had even rolled up his window and leaned over to roll up hers. Siri had never heard him so clearly. He was bursting her eardrums, so she put up a hand to block the ear closest to him. Fool!

"Let's talk about something," he was saying.

"Go ahead."

"What would you like to talk about?"

"Nothing."

"Well," he said, sitting back, "then, I'll talk."

"I can't hear you."

"CAN YOU HEAR ME NOW?" he shouted. "I wasn't happy at your age either."

Siri looked out the window. They were in the country now—no leaves, no grass, just gray field and black trees. I like it like this, she thought.

"ARE YOU HAPPY NOW, DAD!" Siri shouted.

"I'm contented. There's a difference. When you get a little older, you'll understand." He stopped. "Are you enjoying the scenery?"

"What scenery?"

"Tell me what you'll do when you get back. Will Esther be there?"

"I don't want to talk about it," she said, but just the sound of Esther's name spoken by someone who didn't even know her cheered Siri up. She could breathe.

"I hope Teddy doesn't get rabies, but maybe he will," she said, trying it out.

Her father laughed. "Are you rabid?"

"Don't make fun of it," Siri said.

"I'm not going to ask you why you bit your brother, Siri."

"Good."

"Because I know you don't know why."

Was this better or worse? Siri wondered. "It was an impulse," she said. Dusk was approaching and the gray grass and black trees were smoothing out into colorless flats. I like it, she thought. But real darkness brought out the highway lights, with their artificial sparkle.

"Everything's an impulse," she said, wondering if she knew what an impulse was. It sounded something like electricity.

"True enough," her father said.

They lapsed into silence. Siri fell asleep, the sweetest she'd had since summer. Dad had a hard time waking her up, gave in and sat there in the parking lot. How much time went by? He must have seen a hundred cars drive in, park and empty out. His daughter's head was cocked back and her mouth open. The sleeping body gave off rings of heat, but the car was getting cold. Donald was nearly in a trance, but Siri was suddenly awake.

"Hey!" she said, flinging open the door. She was home.

3.

The typewriter was lodged in its case between the two desks. At first Siri planned to rent it to Esther, but when Esther seemed content to bang away on the manual— which Siri gave her—and was writing all the time on it, never put it away, made funny faces that Siri could see from where she lay on her unmade bed, and the manual became like a third roommate whom Esther seemed to prefer to the second, Siri offered the use of the electric. Esther had never used an electric and, since it was quieter and could be freely operated after lights out, and Siri had a ream of "corrasable" onionskin, which she offered as part of the deal, Esther packed up the manual. Siri said the electric was too expensive to be left out collecting dust, so Esther's typing was restricted and the machine lived between the two desks. Typing was worse than reading where Siri was concerned.

Esther and Siri could read together. Siri was a better reader now, and could rest her eyes on a page and move them to the next page without expecting a treat, or falling asleep, or feeling "strangulated," as she put it, by the filling boredom.

Esther had taught her how to tackle those huge blocks of type that came with college textbooks. These paragraphs ran on forever and, by the time you got to the end, you forgot the beginning, and if you went back to check, you lost your place; and if you slowed down, you got tied up in the end of one sentence and the beginning of the next, which was what she meant by "strangulated." Esther said she understood; that was natural. Siri just wasn't reading fast enough to avoid that kind of entanglement.

Reading was speed. You had to do better than keep up with the author, you had to outrun him. This crazy idea made Siri angry and the first reading lessons ended in spats with Esther. But Siri couldn't get the better of someone like Esther. Esther was patient, and Esther was argumentative. She was confident. It was just a matter of time.

How can you get ahead of him, Siri asked, looking up from the biology text that went with the health class, if you don't know what the fool is talking about? And, she added, you don't care.

Esther had no answer to that one, and the subject was dropped, but then she returned to whatever it was she was reading and Siri was alone in the dark, because Esther did her best and longest reading with a flashlight.

The next step was teaching Siri how to read fast by using the egg timer, which Esther had brought back from home in a box of kitchen supplies. The Ferrys were, Siri found out, moving to an apartment as soon as Mr. Ferry retired, so every article Mrs. Ferry had two of was going to Esther for her hope chest. (The roommates laughed at this absurdity, in spite of the fact that Siri already had a hope chest and it was a very nice one, no matter what Esther might think about weddings and trousseaus.) Esther was keeping the practical things (egg beater, potato masher, spoons, pressure cooker and spatula) for when she got her own apartment, which was the first Siri heard about this prospect.

How can you get an apartment of your own, she asked, if we have to live on campus for four years? Plus, she added, in an unusual spurt of thought, there are no apartments around here; this is the country. Esther said she didn't plan to spend four years at St. M's. She was transferring as soon as she had a transcript.

"What about me?" Siri said.

"Yeah," Esther said, "I've thought about that. Do you want to transfer?"

Siri said she didn't know. The whole idea made her head spin.

But it stopped spinning when Esther set the egg timer at three minutes and forced Siri to pay attention. "Start here," she said, opening to the first page of a book called *The Pre-Socratic Philosophers*. "I'm giving you this," she said, "because it's something you know nothing about and neither did I, before I read it. You don't need to know anything to understand it. It's the very, very beginning."

Siri didn't believe her. There was no book on earth you could read "cold," as Esther put it. You always needed to know something. No book rested on nothing, not even children's books, which she remembered liking, especially if she didn't have to read them to herself. There were always words in children's books that you couldn't pronounce or understand because they were from olden days or foreign countries. "Spindle" was such a word in "Cinderella" or "Sleeping Beauty." She still didn't know what a spindle was—not that she cared, now or then. "Tinderbox" was another. She still didn't know why a lamp needed oil, or what they meant by the "tree" of knowledge of good and evil. The Bible was impossible to understand and best forgotten. Luckily, Catholics didn't worry about it beyond a few Bible stories which were clearer and in better English.

The timer was set and at first all Siri could do was listen to the ticking. Esther put the timer under her pillow, but if she strained, Siri could still hear it. Esther had to reset the dial and start over. When she rewound and left the room with the timer, Siri was alone with the book. The subject wasn't an interesting one. She didn't know what the Socratics were, so why would she care about the Pre-? Just holding the book with its sticky library cover was painful. It wasn't heavy, but it wasn't light either. The door swung open to Esther's face. "Read!" she hissed. Siri opened the heavy cover and read the library colophon—at least that made sense; then the date, the title, a lot of small-print garbage, the dedication (who cared!) and the table of contents. Then she opened the door to find Esther sitting on the floor with the egg timer on her lap. She had another book—typical. "Start me over. I just got to the beginning." And Esther being Esther, she did.

Inside Siri refound the page where the table of contents was, flipped past the introduction—never worth reading, even *she* knew that—and onto the half page under the numeral I.

She held the page with a finger and flopped back on the bed, then (fearing instant sleep) sat upright, but now her eyes were itchy, and one was pulsing. Instead of leaping up to look at it in the mirror, she focused both eyes on the line under the I. There was the word "Pre-Socratics" and a short sentence saying who they were.

Siri read it once, then read it again. No, she thought, that was too slow. Esther would already be on chapter 2, so she dropped her eye to the bottom of the page, but that didn't help. Even she could tell that jumping over the paragraph, or slotting through the center was not the same as reading. For one thing, she still didn't know what the paragraph said. Reading down the edges was stupider, because that's where all the small words fell: the ofs, the its, the thises.

So, with half the time eaten up by experiments, Siri read sentence 2, when she refound the end of sentence 1 and put her finger on it. Sentence two was more about sentence one, but made better sense. This was really who the Pre-Socratics were. It told you where they came from and what order they came in. Siri hadn't heard of any of these countries and the names were crazy, but at least there were only five of them and, sure enough, when she went back to the table of contents, there were seven chapters: this one, about all of them, five following about each separately, and a conclusion. Easy enough.

And here was Esther. How far had she gotten? The three minutes were up.

They tried it again.

It was a Saturday, one week later, a mild January day, although a snowstorm was predicted for later when the wind changed and, sure enough, the weak blue sky was already clouding up.

"Tell me something about the Pre-Socratics."

Siri looked at Esther. She knew who they were; she knew she knew and Esther knew she knew.

"Come on," Esther said, "spit it out."

Siri's brain was packed with information about these five Pre-Socratics. She knew their names and Esther explained how the dates got smaller rather than larger as time passed—a stupid idea, but that's the way it was back then. Siri began. Thales was water.

"Good," said Esther.

Heraclitus thought things were all fire.

"Excellent."

In between were the other three guys who picked out the other two items (ground and air) as the basis for all life.

"Good," said Esther, who was listening and reading at the same time.

How could they be so stupid, these Pre-Socratics, was a question that had occurred the first day. At first, Esther thought the question itself a stupid one, but in time, she came to see how Siri saw it, and although it was ignorant and naive, it was not stupid.

"You don't understand what an abstraction is," she said that day.

"Yes, I do," said Siri, sick of being the dumb one, although that had never bothered her before.

"What is it?"

Siri looked at Esther. Her skin was looking better since she'd gone on birth-control pills, which Siri helped her get from a dermatologist recommended by hers. Now that she was working in the cafeteria for spending money, she could afford a real haircut, so the crazy red hair was calmer, but it had its own style which it returned to the day after the stylist worked on it.

Siri discovered that in answering a hard question, it was better to let your mind rest a little, especially if it was crammed with reading. Rest it a little or let it be distracted. Don't force it, and out would come the answer on its own.

"Come on," Esther said, her face screwing up in that funny way that always made Siri laugh.

The laugh did it. "The opposite of concrete is abstraction."

"Good!" said Esther, spinning on one foot, the way she did when Siri "hit the jackpot," about once out of ten or twenty shots.

"That's enough, I've had enough."

Exam week came and went. During the thick of the studying, the Pre-Socratics were put aside with the egg timer. Esther was in the library every spare minute. Sometimes Siri went with her and sat across from her at the big library table whose surface was sticky. The overhead lights beat down on the heads of mostly juniors and seniors. Freshmen studied in their dorm in bathrobe and slippers. Here in the library the studying girls were in sweater sets and snug, boiled-wool jackets. Some of these girls were "pinned" and a handful had engagement rings. Once Esther settled in place, with her notebook and a chewed Bic, Siri was free to study the scene. To Esther, studying was like breathing, but even Esther was afraid of finals and the nervousness, she said, had made her brain porous. She had a good memory, but exams required retention *and* retrieval, she told Siri. She had to be able to stuff it in and pull it out in the right order; leave what you might need later, but clean out what you used and would never need again. Esther's mother was a professional maid—housekeeper, Esther insisted, but maid, housekeeper, what's the difference? She was good at it, much in demand, but at home she was ferocious. Esther didn't know just how ferocious until she left home and heard from rich types like Siri what that kind of mother did on average to keep house. (Siri thought she wouldn't be interested in this subject because she detested housework and never did any, but Esther's description of Mrs. Ferry with mop and pail, broom and vacuum, and the rag she wore on her head was irresistible, and in fact caused Siri to think, even to dream, in ways she never had before about something that didn't concern her.)

Studying for finals, Esther insisted, was exactly like Anna's style of housework. It was intense, killing, ferocious, and when you were finished, you came out of it, Esther said, clean and new, every surface bright and clutter-free.

Siri had to rely on memory to play the mental scenes of Anna attacking a house because these days Esther was too busy note-taking and memorizing to act out the scenes. For the first time, thanks to Esther, Siri had things to think about when there was nothing else going on. She was never—or almost never—bored. She could, in the middle of a quiet and musty reading room, look for hours at the heads and busts of the studying girls, pinned, unpinned, engaged or not, or she could remind herself of what she knew about ancient philosophy (all filed by Esther's system under "Pre-Socratics"—she was almost ready, Esther said, to turn to Plato). Or, best of all, because almost as funny as the Stooges or Laurel and Hardy, she could animate the scenes of Anna "swicking out" a house: using a razor blade (a razor blade!) to clean tile grooves in the bathroom, dabbing bleach on the tire tread that squeezed the door of the fridge, sterilizing pipes under the sink, and (this was the killer, and Siri had to hold both hands over her laughing mouth) washing the bottoms of the artificial fruit in the fruit bowl, and soaking the stems of the artificial flowers; sponging the plastic coats of the "new" (bought in 1958, Esther said, on "time") living room set.

The library nun was tapping Siri on the shoulder and showing her a finger placed on her own lips, and Siri knew from experience that it was best for all that she head back to the dorm before screams and whoops of helpless laughter disturbed the peace of the reading room, crowded, every seat occupied, every cubit of air, as Esther would say, sucked up. "Get me outta here!" she yelled, as soon as the glass doors closed behind her, and then a lifetime of stifled laughter boiled up and out into the frigid night.

She had never felt so good in her life. But why? She was locked up in an all girls prison with no movies or TV or a decent radio station, and no real friends except for Esther, who was more than a friend, but also less. Siri walked in the frosted night on the blacktop, then on the sidewalk of the silent campus. She was nearly dead center, a spot where the whole peasly (hardly bigger than a regional high school) campus could be seen. From here she saw the eerie fly light glimmering on the chapel's stained-glass windows. Gave you the shivers. Above that were the nun's bedrooms, blinds shut and curtains closed (as if anyone would want to look!), and above that, the freshman bedrooms. Hanging on one window, a string of Christmas lights, and on another Valentine hearts pasted on the glass. They made such a big deal over every lousy holiday, it was pathetic. Except for those seniors who got their diamonds for Christmas, who could be bothered decorating when it was just them and the nuns?

The coffee shop (open till eleven this week and next) was packed and smoke hovered over the tables. Siri bought a package of little donuts and a mint tea and found a table near the door, where the light wasn't as sharp. She had, among her school books, *Emma* and the Pre-Socratics, and for the first time (call the ambulance!) she wanted to read, and not just to prove something to Esther, who wasn't even there to time her or to check afterwards to see what she remembered. It was a question of which book. Novels were fun and this one was really fun, but Siri liked the company of the Pre-Socratics with their simple patter. They decided what was what, then made their observations. Whether this was inductive or deductive, Siri didn't know. This was the very latest thing Esther was trying to pound into her head but, as with Bovary, Siri liked the facts and the details. Categories were of no interest.

What she liked about Thales and Heraclitus (whose names rolled right off her tongue) was their simplicity (a new word and so much better than "simple," or stupid or naive or primitive, all of which could be applied to these two, and the other three, but why call them names when they'd been dead for so long; what good could the criticism do?). "Simplicity," wrote Siri on the top of a clean page of her daybook. She was on page 2. Underneath—because Esther was breaking her into Plato and some of his notions before she cracked that one—were "simphonium" and "fado," and under that "ideals" and "ideas." Esther said these were different, but notice the root they had in common. Siri could see the root, and Esther had said the root was Greek.

And here was Dotty Votta, asking if she'd like to play a hand of poker. It was nice to be asked, but no thank you. Dotty's group wasn't even that good at cards and Siri had to explain things to them—a first. (She heard herself in those moments sounding like a nagging Sybele and cut it short on the spot, but word got out that Siri Sorenson was an ace at five-card stud.)

"Water," she wrote under MONISM, and under water, THE ONE. "Fire," she wrote on the right-hand side. "All things are full of gods." History test was tomorrow. Esther had read—she wasn't bragging; it was just a fact—the western civ text, chapters 1–10, three times. There were pages she could recite from memory. Siri didn't believe it, but pick a page, Esther said, with a main topic, and Siri did. Then Esther, with little prompting, spilled out a few paragraphs. She could even describe the picture or graph, if there was one.

Siri hadn't read these chapters even once. She had skimmed them. "What does skim mean to you?" Esther asked.

Siri was getting used to these questions and to taking

them seriously. She stopped what she was doing (putting on hand cream) and gazed at the ceiling. She relaxed her gaze until the perforations (soundproofing, Esther called it) blended into streaks. Skimming. To skim. Was skin milk, skim milk? Or was skim milk, skin milk? That thought pierced her brain, and she followed it through.

"Sorenson!" Esther said.

"I'm thinking."

What did skimming have to do with the bulky history textbook, all five million knee-crushing pages of it?

"Hurry up," Esther said. "I've got cafeteria duty in fifteen minutes."

"Skimming," Siri said, with her eyes shut, "is to history—"

"Good," said Esther, "you're using the analogy form."

"Skimming," Siri repeated, and what then came to mind was blinding in its face. "It means nothing."

"What do you mean it means nothing?"

"I mean that even if I skimmed, which I didn't because I didn't even open all the pages flat—"

Esther sighed.

"By skimming I mean flipping. Is that the right word, Esther, for taking all the pages and letting them blow over or flop over from one hand to the other?"

"Flipping," Esther said, "yeah, I get it."

"Well," Siri went on, with her eyes shut tight. "Skimming means opening every page and letting your eyes touch all the lines, or least the headlines. And even *that*—" she said.

"Yeah?"

"—is not enough to know the history, especially if it's all new to you."

"If you were going to skim—" Esther said. "Now listen—if you were going to skim in time to take the history test on Monday, how long would it take and how much time should you set aside?"

"How many pages?"

Esther reached for the book. "Four hundred twenty-one, but some of them are half a page."

"I don't know. I've never skimmed anything before."

"Should I get the egg timer?"

That was Saturday, and today was Sunday. Esther had the western civ book in the library because Siri planned the skimming for the hours right before the test. She didn't know how long it would take, and neither did Esther.

Esther had warned that waiting till the hours right before the test might work for history, but it didn't leave any time to cram for biology, which came right after history, and for the two tests that fell on the next day.

Siri didn't want to think that far ahead. That was asking too much. The pleasure she felt in knowing the hours from midnight till nine were set aside, banked, if you will, for the skimming of history, was intense, a new feeling of security, plus confidence. And it depended on no one else but herself and those hours stored up in the bank.

She opened the Pre-Socratics. She had time for them. Esther was right: they were the real beginning. Nothing came before them. Each sentence they wrote was pure and separate; they were like the sentences in primary school books. "See Spot run." Those were the days when Siri liked reading: words and pictures were the same and an equal number on each page.

"It's death for souls to become wet." That was one. "The road up and the road down are one and the same." "A fool is excited by every word." That's what Heraclitus said, and he was right.

Siri took the trouble to copy each of these sentences, one to a page, leaving room for commentary. She had two and a half sentences written when Esther showed up to pass on the history book. Esther opened the donuts ("You shouldn't let me eat these") and took a sip of the cold mint tea. "What are you writing?"

Siri cleared her throat. "A fool," she read, "is excited by every word."

Esther laughed.

"At first, I didn't know what this meant."

"Read me what you wrote about it."

"'We think,'" Siri read, "'we know what we mean by the word fool.'"

"You sound like a philosopher, Siri."

Siri went on: "'And maybe we do.'" She looked up.

"That's all you have?"

"That's it for that one."

"'And maybe we do'?"

"And maybe we do."

"Cool. I'm starting to get it. 'And maybe we do.'"

"I'm tired now. Let's go back to the dorm. I'm going to bed."

They walked under the cold stars. Esther said, "You can't go to bed."

"Why not?"

"You've got to skim!"

Siri was on probation. That's what the note from the dean said. A copy was sent home and she'd hear from them when they got it and saw the report card: two Fs, two Ds and a C. The C was in history. The skimming had worked and the C meant more to the roommates—and even the hallmates—than all Esther's As and even her A+. Siri was a scholar; she might even be a genius if she could ace the test on five hours of skimming pages she'd never seen before.

"What do you mean," Siri said, "'ace'?"

"A, Siri. You had to get an A on that to make a C, going in with what you had."

"You mean all those quizzes?"

"The quizzes and the term paper."

"I don't remember the term paper."

"Don't you remember the thing you did on the twelve Caesars?"

"No."

"Remember we set them up in a panel discussion as if they were all alive at the same time?"

"Vaguely. Did you write it?"

"That was when we were using the manual."

"Oh."

"You don't remember. I can see you don't. How can you forget? We were up for two nights in a row."

"The twelve Caesars?"

"Julius, Octavian, Nero, Claudius, Caligula—"

"Oh yeah, I remember. What did I get on it?"

"I don't know, but it wasn't a good grade."

"Whose fault was that?"

"I had my own paper to write, don't forget. All I could do was correct yours. It was funny how you had them talking. They sounded like gangsters."

"Weren't they?"

"See, Siri. Do you see now? You've got a brain just like everyone else."

"Oh, shut up."

The skimming was the craziest night Siri had ever spent that didn't involve a fight with Sybele or a backseat tussle with some grubby boy.

What was it like? Esther asked because, after the first hour, consisting of tears, the pep talk, the Coke break, Esther was asleep. If she didn't get some sleep, the "material," as she called it, squeezed into her brain, wouldn't cook and come out in clean chunks worthy of credit.

To teach Siri how to skim, the two girls sat together on Siri's bed with their backs against the headboard and overhead lights blazing.

Together they read—or skimmed—the prehistoric eons. The big book was already underlined from Esther's work, so Siri should circle the things she wanted to remember. "Don't bother with my marks," Esther told her. "You'll never remember all that."

"Get one fact straight," she went on, "then you can fill in the rest with the skims."

Siri looked puzzled.

"Pull out one sentence on the Iron Age, say——"

"Which one?"

"Well, find one I've underlined—like this," Esther said, finding a sentence shaded in by the textbook company and double-underlined by Esther. "See, here's the pith.

"Write it down or memorize it, one or the other. Then, skim the next few pages so your eye picks out one or two details or examples. Make sure, though, that you're still reading about the Iron Age. That's what these titles are for. Everything under one of these titles is the same subject. Pick a sentence, skim. Next heading. Pick out a sentence, skim."

It sounded easy, but when you tried to do it for 20 pages, let alone 421, it was impossible, so instead, as two o'clock turned into three, and Siri's tired eyes formed dark tunnels where letters blended and lines ran together, there was only one thing to do: look at the pictures, read the captions and "connect the dots," as Esther would say.

Did it work? Must have, because Siri wrote for an hour and a half, the longest she'd ever held a pen in her hand. The exam was slated for three hours, and even that wasn't enough time, Esther had said afterwards, but Siri was done first, and delivered her blue book (Esther handed in three) to the proctor.

If that were history, she knew it cold, and it was a cinch, and it was, she told Esther, wasn't it? I don't know, Esther admitted, because I don't know what you wrote down. Which questions did you answer?

Siri had skipped the hundred multiple-choice and matchups (too detailed), and hit the essays, but the questions were too involved and took too long to read, so she wrote her own essay. "Why are you so surprised?" she said, seeing Esther's face. "What's wrong with that?"

"What was your essay about?"

"The Pre-Socratics," Siri said. "Aren't they part of it?"

4.

Winter was turning into spring, but spring was grudging. One day, the air was luscious: warm and seed-scented, the next cold and raw. The greens of flowers appeared in the beds in front of Great Hall, but the rare, colored bud, the early bird, froze and rotted. Spring term cleared out some of the old courses and a new set of books mingled with the old. For Siri, the old was everything but history. She'd wanted a clean sheet and had earned it, but Esther convinced her to stick with history. Otherwise, she'd end up with a big gap after the Middle Ages. But, said Siri, looking at a timeline, the gap started earlier. Her gap started before the Classical Age really got going, let alone the Roman Age, the fall of Rome, the Dark Age (Huns and Barbarians versus Catholics), and the time that Esther was calling the Middle Ages, which was the point where Mr. Whitman ended part 1 and began, in the spring term, with part 2. Part 2 was the Middle Ages to 1945. They were plowing though the middle right now, and it was unbelievably complicated, yet filled with comic characters: William the Orange, Henry the Eight, Richard the Lion, Joan of Arc, Mary the Scot, Magna Carta, Catherine the Russian. No one had a last name. It was like the old days when telephone numbers still had letters and zip codes were one number. Even Siri could see that history, as it tumbled forward, took something conveniently small and made it huge and impersonal. These Middle Agers didn't live very long, even if they were rich—that's what Siri could figure out on her own. Their houses were not clean or warm—not even the castles—and the streets weren't paved or blacktopped, no matter what the history books said about the good quality of the Roman roads. There was no birth control, so marriage automatically meant having twelve or more, or dying in childbirth. Some girls married at twelve, or even eight, and they were having babies before they had their height. Travel was miserable. Rubber had not been discovered, nor had electric lights or anything with a battery. What was life like then? Siri wondered, after reading a page about the Age of Exploration and the clipper ships. Lousy. Esther agreed that it was miserable, and not only agreed, but came to Siri, who'd thought so long and hard about "living conditions," with questions. Esther could memorize, but didn't have time for visualizing or filling in the blanks, with the six courses she was taking so that she could graduate in three years. That way she wouldn't need to transfer. Visualizing was the fun of it, Siri told her, and, on sleepless nights, when it was warmish and they lay awake smelling the blanket of seedy air and manured earth, they visualized. Sometimes Siri started with "once upon a time," and sometimes Esther gave a date and some facts and Siri worked to create a "tableau."

"What did they eat?" was always Esther's first question to Siri, because at midnight, six hours after supper, they were hungry.

Mead was what they drank. It was like wine, only tasted

more like beer with a little honey. The mead was thick and came out of jars. Even the cups they used in those days had no handles and were beady or gritty on the sides. Mead could make you very drunk, so women and children drank it watered down. There was also water in huge jars which, remember, Jesus had them turn into wine, but this was long after his time, so water stayed water and it was not cold or iced.

"No ice?" Esther asked, even though this was something she knew.

"They had fruit juice."

"They did?"

"They crushed grapes with their feet and that was just as good for juice as for wine."

"Was there milk?"

"People didn't drink milk then."

"What'd they do with it?"

"They cooked with it."

"On campfires?"

"Fireplace. Milk was used for tapioca and porridge."

"Porridge is oatmeal."

"It's oatmeal that's left out to harden in the pot."

Siri supplied these pictures of life, using "data" from the history book and some extra skimming, but Mr. Whitman had told them to come into Boston and take a look at the medieval art in the museums there. They could see how far off they were.

"Some of their art is still around?" Siri asked Esther.

"Spoons, utensils, vases. It was left in the churches. The ones that weren't burned down or bombed."

"They had bombs!"

Esther didn't know when bombs came in, but it was after the Middle Ages.

Esther had grown an inch since September and thinned out once she started skipping breakfast. She was taller than Siri and still growing. She had decided on English as a major. It wasn't easy to pick because she was good at everything. Siri had talked her out of physics and chemistry. What differ- ence was there between that and what her father did for a living. The whole idea of education was being free not to work with your hands.

"How do you know?" Esther asked. "Who do you know who works with their hands?"

Siri thought for a minute. "Jesus's father, Joseph of Ari- mathea."

Esther laughed. "I've never heard him called that. But you're wrong," Esther added. "Physics is done entirely in people's heads."

"No, it isn't. It happens on a lab table."

"Well, the math part happens in the head. There are no lab tables for math."

"Math is practical. And practical is blue-collar."

"Siri!" Esther said. "What do you know about 'blue-col- lar'?"

"I know what it is."

"Okay, tell me what you've heard about it."

"Christo's dad repairs TVs. That's blue."

"That's not blue, Siri."

"Yes, it is so."

"No, it is not. Blue means wearing a dark uniform—blue, gray, sometimes brown, to do dirty work."

"It doesn't have to be a uniform, Esther. It can just be some shirt that gets filthy on the job."

"I'm not sure you're right."

"Well, I *am* sure."

"What should I major in then?"

"Something fun. You're going to end up spending four years doing it."

"I'm going to spend the rest of my life doing it."

Siri was lying on the bed reading a book on Plato. Her major—no questions asked—would be philosophy. She had no interest in anything else. She put a finger in the book to hold her place. "Aren't you going to get married?"

"Marriage isn't a career."

"I know. You told me. But still. Are you going to work your whole life?"

"Why not?"

Siri reopened her book and found the tricky sentence she'd been reading and rereading. It was annoying, but the more she picked at these sentences, the clearer Plato was becoming. Plato wasn't as hard as people said, especially since his friends made him explain everything and they always started from nowheresville The commentaries were hard because they weren't conversations at all, but Siri was sure she understood Plato better than any boring critic. Sometimes it was fun to see what dumbbells they were. None of them were paying attention. They were like the fools in Heraclitus, who were excited by every word. They were so excited, they went right off track. Thinking this was so enjoyable that Siri forgot to listen to what Esther was saying. Esther had taught Siri, after the reading lessons were finished, how to read and do something else at the same time—like have a conversation and listen to a lecture—but Siri still wasn't good at it. She was so good at reading that everything else came second, or fell off.

"Are you listening to me?"

"Yup."

"What do you think I should major in?"

"English," Siri said, just to get Esther to stop talking; and it would, she knew, because Esther hadn't taken a single English course, except for composition. It was a bolt from the blue.

"Okay," Esther said, half an hour later. "I'll be an English major."

Esther went to the English advisor, a man, but nothing like Mr. Whitman, who was spending less time on campus because his dissertation was due. The advisor, Dr. Timothy Farrand, was reading a newspaper, but not the *Globe* or the *Herald*. Esther didn't recognize the paper; it was pink. What she told Siri, when Siri came back from meeting the philosophy advisor, was that English had built himself a nice little nest in the basement of Great Hall. On his side table were a tea set and a hotplate. His desk had a bowl of flowers and an ink pot. Pictures of writers on the walls—photos in black frames—and every inch of wall space filled with books, all tidy and even on the shelves. An oriental rug—or doghouse rug, as Esther put it to Siri, to remind her that they were speaking of a room no bigger than a closet or a lavette—under his feet.

Siri put her book down, hearing in Esther's tone that there was more to this. Esther was leaning against the wall, flushed, with curly hair damp at the edges. Now she whirled in front of the mirror, evaluating something in it, or just turning her back so Siri couldn't see her face.

"I'm listening," Siri said, tossing the book on the floor.

"That's all,"Esther said. "I'm going to the library."

"Look at me," Siri said, but Esther still faced the mirror. "What happened?"

Dr. Farrand was thirty-one. Esther knew, because it was his birthday. He told me, Esther said, because I was the first student to come to his office all year.

Siri laughed. "Did he sign you up for English?"

"He said I should think about it. English takes real commitment, he said, much more than science."

"That's baloney," said Siri, who knew the difference even after one semester in college.

"It's like a religious vocation, he said. No different from being a nun or a priest, except—"

"Except what?"

"You don't have the benefit of an order, or money from the pope, or people to take care of you."

"Weird," Siri said, thinking she might visit this doctor, too. "Did you tell him about reading *The Second Sex* in French?"

"I mentioned it."

"What'd he say?"

"He said not to waste time on politics. I told him my roommate was a philosopher."

"Was he impressed?"

"No. He said, compared to English, philosophy was like the Girl Scouts."

"Where is he?" said Siri, kicking her feet on the bed. "I'll kill him."

Esther laughed. "He won't talk to you. He reserves his time for English and English only."

The interview convinced Esther. Philosophy was advised by a nun and that was enough for Siri, especially since this nun taught all the courses: ancients and moderns, epistemology and metaphysics, phenomenology and logic. There were three courses offered. The courses were there to support theology, which wasn't a major either, except for the girls who planned on "entering." What could you do with theology? Teach CCD? Work in the rectory? There was no future in it for girls. Even "religious," the nun explained, didn't need that much theory. They relied on priests for that.

"She was a funny old bird," Siri said.

"In what way?"

"She asked whether I had a boyfriend. What did my dad do for a living, and where had my mother grown up. She thought she might remember Sybele because she'd been here twenty-five years ago. She said Sybele must have been a 'social butterfly.'"

"Poor thing," said Esther. "I guess no one comes to see her either."

Esther signed up for English courses, but there was a problem: where would she get the books? Siri had no major, since there was no real philosophy at St. M's, and she was taking a half load by special exemption. That way, the dean had explained, her Fs would be "forgiven." That was the word she used, and Siri didn't like the sound of it. "Don't fight it," Esther had warned.

Besides history, Siri was enrolled in College English, a pre-major course given in the English Department, but the books for CE were useless for the things Esther was taking: Milton, medieval poetry, Chaucer and the metaphysicals. Esther had gone to the bookstore with a paper and pen. The total cost of these books (hardcover and paper) was more than a hundred dollars. "Why don't you sell something?" Siri said.

"Like what?"

"I don't know. Why don't you sell something to me? I could get a check from my father for next year's birthday. He'll never know. Or, I'll say it's for 'carfare,' or I want to join the museum like you're always promising me we're going to do."

"What should I sell you?"

"I don't know. What do you have that you think I'd like?"

Esther looked around the room. "What about *The Second Sex* in French?"

"Isn't that Mr. Whitman's book?"

"Oh yeah." Esther looked around, then said: "What do you want to learn next? I could sell you some lessons?"

"What could you teach me?"

Siri was interested. The reading had been a success. She had never read a whole book in her life and now she had read three, cover to cover, and parts of three others, including a chapter of the English *Second Sex,* which was all philosophy, but still went over her head. Esther said she needed to work up to it. That Beauvoir's philosophy— which was really Sartre's—came very late, and a lot of other things came before—Descartes, Spinoza, Hegel. These were the names she remembered from reading Father Copleston. Philosophy, Esther explained, was like a family where father taught son and everything was passed on, just like the Pre-Socratics had taught each other, and then Socrates, who taught Plato. It was tidy, just like a string, unlike the mess of English and the hellhole of detail that was history.

Esther was still thinking. "I could teach you to write. I could also teach you to think."

"I could teach *you* to think," Siri said.

"Well, I could still teach you to write."

"Do you agree that I could teach you how to think?" Siri asked Esther, studying her face to see the answer before Esther could change it. "Answer me."

"I'm not sure I know what you mean by thinking."

"I don't know what I mean, but aren't I pretty good at whatever it is?" Siri said, remembering the Pre-Socratics and Plato, and how hard a simple thing could be and how long it would take to unravel all the threads. "Aren't I better than you?"

Esther reflected. "At some things, yes, at some thinking, yes. Yes, you are."

Siri screamed with delight, leaping up on the bed to jump.

Esther said it, and she meant it.

"Teach me to write," Siri said. "Use my charge at the bookstore."

"I'll buy secondhand books," Esther said.

"I don't care what you buy."

Taking a half load, and one of them a baby course, Siri had time to read Plato and to write, and there was still time left over. She used it to rest. Being so thin and never sleeping, she caught two colds in a row and the second evolved into bronchitis and the threat of isolation in the convent infirmary. No one wanted to go there, no matter how sick they were, so Siri hid her sickness even from Esther. She held back her deepest, sludgiest coughs until Esther was asleep and then hacked them into the pillow until the pillow was soaked. Or ran into the bathroom and turned the hot water on. But walking to CE one day, a cough came on that dredged so deep into the well of mucus that Siri began to choke, and inhaled it, and couldn't breathe or talk, or even scream, and no Esther—in her Chaucer class—so Siri went down and over into a bush. When she opened her eyes, she was lying on the cold sidewalk with scratched face and hands, a ring of faces looking down at her.

It was either the infirmary or the hospital, they were say-ing. She was a very sick girl and she didn't want to infect the whole freshman class, did she?

Siri cried. She wanted to talk to Esther. Where was Esther?

It was the infirmary, and the college doctor was called in. "You belong in the hospital, young lady," he said, after listening to her chest, "but I'd be afraid to move you in the shape you're in."

Siri just wanted to sleep, even in these rough, convent sheets and scratchy, wool blanket, with her head raised on a stack of bricklike pillows to keep the snot from choking her, but first the doctor gave her a penicillin booster and said he'd be back to give her another. Even if it was the flu, he said, the piggyback infections were in her ears and chest, and at least they could roll those back. The booster was painful. Siri cried, but the hot tears brought a slackening of muscles, a release, a sheathing of nerves that lowered her into a sleep as fortified as a coma. In the comalike sleep, Siri rested for the first time in months. As she slid down the soft, yielding slopes, she was caught in a snag: what if she forgot everything she'd learned? She felt like screaming but there was no air, and down the slope she went, despairing, then out cold.

Siri slept for a night and part of the next day. The fever broke on Wednesday and the sickroom nun, Sister Monica, who rarely left the convent, took the chance to nap, but insisted on having it in the cubicle with her patient. Sister was a snorer and the noise woke up Siri. She'd been awake for short spurts, but mostly at night, and she didn't aggravate her misery by asking hard questions like: where am I? or, how did I get here? Whatever covering the last set of malarial dreams offered, she accepted, and slipped back under their protection, borrowing a detail and a bit of dreamy logic to ease the transition.

But the light streaming into the whitewashed sickroom with its ammoniac scent, and the zoo sounds coming from the chair, broke her concentration and the dream thread was snapped. Questions paraded out that would not retreat. Where was she?

But Sister, hearing or sensing a change, was awake and ready to chat and rejoice, dying to tell her charge how much she loved her like her own child and how many prayers, rosaries and Masses had been offered up for just this day's miracle.

Siri shut her eyes, but there was no escape. Sister Monica pulled her chair up close, cranked the bed up and was going to sponge bathe her charge. She had so much to say and they had hours before Doctor's visit.

Sister Monica was the dumbest person Siri had ever met. She wanted to talk, but she had nothing to say. She licked her lips, chapped and shapeless; she cleared her throat. Then she said what she'd already said: how she'd prayed and offered up her daily Mass, even though Doctor had said don't worry, Patient will pull through. "I'm still sick," Siri croaked, closing her eyes on the nun's eager face. She was ageless, as they all were, but with a white "mustache" and eyebrows. When the nun had strained for further conversation and none came, she rolled up her sleeves and wrung out a sour-smelling sponge. "The water's too cold!" Siri shrieked, before a drop touched her skin, and Monica fetched off with the basin. Siri got up and locked the door behind her.

Peace. Siri estimated the time of exile at less than a week and more than a day. Thinking made her head spin. The room was too bright. She threw the covers over her head and ignored the knocks and pitiful arguments from outside. They had keys. Let them search.

Thinking was vertigo, but boredom was worse and Siri, bored her whole life, was ready to scream with boredom, but also with weirdness. Dreams, nightmares, sweats and panics and crushing sadness had made the nights into a circus and part of the days, too. Waking life in this clinic was a monism of boredom, but across the divide of sleep was this new territory—a yawning pit of threats and danger. In a life of boredom and idleness, Siri Sorenson had been spared (or denied) this rich spoilage of fancy. Those days were over.

Siri had—just last night—attended the Symposium at Athens, and walked with the peripatetics, but it wasn't what you might think. They were all monkeys and fools, and the sheets they wore for clothes were ragged and yellow, wrinkled and food-stained. These sheets dragged on the floor, tripping up the ones behind. They all talked at once, or coughed and choked, told fortunes and played cards. That was one dream, easy enough to ignore if more hadn't followed. Esther was in most of them. Sometimes Esther looked like Sybele, and vice versa.

When Esther and Sybele were both there, they had dialogues, but Siri couldn't break into them, even when she had something to say. It was worse than being ignored. It was annihilation, and—sure enough—the pain of it broke the dream's shell, and opened another sideshow.

Such were the nights of illness. Waking moments were tidal pools of weakness, made for crying or coughing, a soup of pain and tedium. Today was the first sharp clearing, and Siri wasn't going to waste it on Monica, or on the doctor, either. She was free and freedom was the condition of a conscious being, the thing-for-itself, or—as Esther liked to say—the thing they both could be if Siri would only try a little harder.

One thing was the first thing, and this had been hovering with the sickness for weeks, even months: she, Siri, had nothing going for her. She was not smart (like Esther), not strong (like Monica, for instance); she had just learned to read, at a point where other girls were set to put reading aside for adult pursuits; she had failed almost all her first-term classes, and missed many hours of the new, reduced load (College English and History after the Middle Ages). She had no friends but Esther, and how long would that last if Esther planned to graduate in two and a half years? She had only the money her father gave her and her mother would leave her and Teddy—if it wasn't already spent by them on cars, decorators and shrinks.

She was beautiful—or used to be. (How did she know for sure? Who and what had given evidence? Dad? What did he know? Mother, who only saw what reminded her of herself? Boys? They couldn't be dumber and what pool did they have to judge from? The mirror? There was no mirror in the cubicle. She had to remember. What color hair? Her driver's license said light brown, but Sybele insisted it was blond. One cancelled out the other: it was neither. Siri pulled a lank strand in front of her eyes: it was limp, greasy and the color of a paperbag. Go on, she told herself, taking the belligerent tone that Esther took with everything that presented itself for judgment. [Siri missed Esther and was turning herself into Esther to have her around. How funny that was—funny, yes, but not in a way that anyone would understand.] Eyes were green, but you could also say snot or gray, or the color of sandbags. Skin used to be pink and thick and smooth and everyone wanted to touch it, even strangers, but—looking at an arm to see—now it had no color at all, a little greenish, and the arm so skinny, the flesh hung a little off the bone, and the muscle looked like a clothesline. No figure. It had always been boyish—svelte, Dad would say; whippet, Christo, who had a good vocabulary for a boy.)

The nuns had found the key. Monica burst in the door, with the doctor behind her. "Time to go back to school," he said, although the big syringe was already out of his bag with a promise of two more in the days to come.

Monica wanted to help her dress. "Get out," Siri said, adding, "Sister Monica," because one thing she knew: don't make an already bad thing worse. "Please," she added, for a safety margin.

"Oh, let me," Sister said, but Siri shook her head, pointing to the door. It was a new life. Start here with nothing but the clothes she walked in (or was dragged in) with.

Siri wobbled down the convent corridor, smelling of wax and pitchpine. There was an old-lady smell, too, but don't pursue it, she told herself, or any of the other faint odors that signified the sacrifices these women had made, and for what? And with that, Siri almost slid to the floor. Did "for what?" mean what she thought it meant? "For what?" she whispered, and halted, waiting for an answer, or just to catch her breath. Her own dad, not a Catholic and not even a good Protestant, had accused Siri's "generation"—whatever that meant—of being "faithless."

"I believe in God, the Father Almighty," Siri burbled, trying it out. She said it again, mumbled it. It was still nothing, less than nothing, more monotonous than the plain equations of simpletons like Thales and Anaximander. It was still the Dark Ages if these crones had given up even the pathetic life Sybele had, with a house and a few new appliances, a new car every spring, for this dowdy convent reeking of Pine-Sol and deadly routine: round-the-clock prayer, a standard of conduct—be meek and ordinary and look out for everyone else but yourself; stifle your anger and lust (what lust?)—and all for what?

Keep moving, Siri told her stiff legs. The floor was slippery and her flats skated along, not one inch from the floor. Siri was skin and bones, but her legs were lead and she had the feet of an elephant. Slip-sliding home, stripped of faith—if she had ever really had any—and with her personal value at zero, she arrived at the door of the room shared with Esther. She stood there and checked the number, then knocked.

She had to knock again, because no answer. She turned the knob and there was Esther, face flat in her pillow, dressed with her shoes on. (What day was it? Saturday? Sunday?) "Hey," said Siri, who could see that Esther had her own story—and more dramatic than self-annihilation, or so it looked. The room was a mess, clothes on the floor, some still on their hangers; powder spilled on the dresser, and Siri's bed torn apart. The sheets and quilt looked like they'd been in a tornado. "Jesus Marion Joseph!" Siri said, quoting Esther, quoting her father. "Hey," she said. "Get up!"

Esther was crying. No, she was laughing. Maybe it was both. "Hey," Siri said for the third time, and finally, the girl rolled onto her back. She was laughing, but it wasn't funny, whatever it was, because Esther looked pale and purple at the same time. Her hair was a bee's nest, and her eyes were bloodshot, yet glinting. Was it eye makeup? It looked like she'd been in an accident, except for the Halloween grin, exposing her teeth to the roots. Were her gums bleeding?

"Did you bite your tongue?" Siri asked.

"What?"

"Never mind," said Siri, dropping onto the bed the tornado had hit.

"Are you better?"

Siri didn't answer, and that established something of the old rapport. Esther sighed.

"Don't sigh."

"I can't help it."

"Help it."

Esther launched her head and neck off the bed.

"Don't stare at me," Siri said, "and, by the way, you don't look so great yourself."

Esther dropped back on the bed.

"What day is it?"

"I don't know."

"You don't know!" Siri said, launching herself up. "Is it a school day, or not?"

"It's not a school day. I think it's Sunday. Aren't those chapel bells?"

Siri listened. "I don't know. Don't they ring every day?"

"Do they?"

"Do they! What's wrong with you?" Siri dropped down again. "No, don't tell me. I've been very sick. I'm weak."

"*I'm* weak."

"Are you sick?"

There was no answer, so Siri asked again. "Are you?" There was no answer, so "Say something!" Siri said.

Esther cleared her throat.

"Go ahead."

"I'm trying." Esther sighed. "And don't tell me not to sigh, because that's all I can do."

Siri lifted her aching head to look. "I don't believe it," she said.

"What?"

"You're in love, aren't you, you stupid ass!"

Siri counted on her fingers. Two, at most three days had passed. If it was Sunday and she'd dropped on Wednesday or Thursday, a half week had passed. And given Esther, that stupid fool of an ass, enough time to wreck everything. And for what?

"Don't try to talk me out of it."

"I haven't said anything."

"You don't have to. You called me a stupid ass, didn't you?"

"You *are* in love!"

"What if I am," Esther said, folding her hands on her stomach which, incidentally, was covered by one of Siri's silk blouses, and if Esther had gotten a stain on it, or something—

"I'm too sick for this," Siri said, with a hand over her forehead. "I'm burning up."

"So am I," said Esther in a tiny, weak voice that Siri had never before heard, and never wanted to hear again.

"You stupid, stupid ass," she said, and now Esther was crying.

"Don't turn on me. Don't move out," she said. "Don't leave me. You're my only friend."

Was this true? Even if it weren't, Siri liked the sound of it. She had the command of another life. She had won the loyalty of someone not a family member. She was not alone, a loser or completely bankrupt. There was Esther and Esther would be loyal for life. Unless—Esther was churning out a heavy volume of thoughts, trying to justify, Siri figured, the fool-ass leap of faith into emotional slavery, paralysis of the will—she were more loyal to some else.

"Esther, stop talking!"

"What?"

Siri halted her talk by raising a hand, fingers flat and firm, blocking the sight of Esther's talking face. She was having a flood of ideas herself, and each was strong, wild and breathtaking. Although tired and still viral, she was more alive than ever. The things coming out of her mind were unrecognizable. She barely had the words to cover them—some of them were too weird to ever find suitable clothes.

Was it Plato? Was it college? Just being here and sitting in the library, watching people study?

"What? Say," Esther said, confirming the reality of the thoughts. What reality? That Siri's scrawny, colorless face (she'd seen it in the dresser mirror) had on it the look of intelligent life.

"I am," she said, "thinking things I've never thought before."

"Great! Just like I told you."

"No," Siri said, holding up the silencing hand. "It has nothing to do with you. Not this." The thoughts had to be preserved, even if they couldn't be spelled out. How? Esther would know. "Help me."

"Help you what?"

"Help me say it."

"Say what?"

"What I'm thinking."

Esther rose and sat on the bed next to Siri. She studied her face, all emaciated, tiny, with the bones of a bird. She looked into her tired, bleary eyes. The girl wanted encouragement, and Esther wanted to give it. "Come on," she said. "Try."

"I can't."

"Try hard, Sear. Bring it up."

Siri closed her eyes, but that made her dizzy. "In my head—"

"Yeah?"

"I can see it all."

"What?"

"Where you're going, Esther, and who you're going with."

Even though Esther was in love and eager to talk, this was a disappointment. Who cared if Siri could see this? She tried to keep the disappointment from showing, but Siri spotted it. She fell back on the bed and covered her eyes.

"Tell me," Esther said. "I want to hear."

"No, you don't. You're already bored."

"It's my life. How could I be bored?"

"It's not good enough. I know. Well, it doesn't matter because I've forgotten it anyway."

"No, you haven't. You still remember."

Siri opened her eyes. "You're involved with that creepy English guy and you've already had sex with him, or all but. And it's as if, Esther, it's as if—" Siri hesitated to get it right. "It's as if—"

"Go on."

"You know. As if you've given up, because you might as well. This guy—I haven't even met him—isn't going to let you—"

"Isn't going to let me what?"

"He isn't. Your life is over."

"You're crazy."

"Maybe so, but your life is still over."

Esther was quiet. She started tidying up the room that passion had wrecked. She hung Siri's silk blouse in the closet.

"Let it air," Siri said, and so Esther brought it out again and hung it on the windowsill. She made the bed and wrapped one of Siri's summer robes (seersucker) around her now-slim frame. "You could be right," she said.

"You know I'm right."

"You haven't even heard the story yet. How do you know?"

"I know."

"How?"

Siri thought: how do I know? "How *do* I know?" she asked Esther.

"Maybe because your mind is a clean slate with just a little ancient philosophy in it and Madame Bovary. Don't forget her. Hey!" Esther said. "*That*'s how you know!"

Siri lay back on the sheets knotted with the quilt, a painful bed, but better than self-support, which she wasn't fully capable of. The bed was mountain and valley and something harder, sharper. There was a shoe! And—reaching into the slurry—a book and even a pencil. "Why'd you do this to my bed?" she asked. "Let me get on yours while you fix mine."

"Okay. Don't forget what you were going to say."

"I've said enough. It's time for you to talk. Now that we understand, or *I* understand, let's enjoy it."

Esther laughed. "You did a lot of growing up in that infirmary. What did they give you, truth serum?"

Siri crawled into Esther's bed with her face to the wall. Esther started to tell the story and, contented, Siri was soon asleep.

"It happened like this," Esther said, but when she started telling it, and before she knew Siri was asleep, the story lost its shape. In Siri's ears—even though she was asleep—it didn't amount to a hill of beans. The memory was dazzling, a gorgeous historical pageant of gowns and high-stepping steeds. Night fell sharp and day dawned shadowless. An indescribable music reformulated the air. Things said resounded as if in a deep well. In Esther's mind, the picture—already matchless—improved. It was perfection and there had been nothing to prepare her for its arrival.

But as the crippled, homemade words tumbled out (words that Anna Ferry could use, and did, just as well),

and as these asinine, half-dead words struck the ear of a listener (Siri), with only Madame Bo and the ancients as brain
food, and dropped into that empty bowl of bourgeois girl-
hood (Sybele and hot rollers and crêpe suzettes and sweater
sets), the drama leaked out of its every hole. What drama?

As Esther reflected, she heard the light snore of slumber,
sighed and slipped into the tumbled bed to finish the story
for herself. And up it came, smaller to start with, but trem-
bling with potential.

Dr. Farrand sat behind his desk in a dark, tweedy jacket,
wafting a slight camphor smell. Dr. Farrand, Esther
repeated, then said it again, until it rang in her ears. His
small, smooth hands were draped over the twin red volumes, which Esther could see were the Loeb *Aeneid*—and
even if she couldn't see, he had told her this when her gaze
fell on them, and on his hands. She could feel her face
flaming. The hands opened a volume and he read. There
was some point he was making and the evidence for it was
there under his fingers, but Esther could no more remember the point than lift her eyes off the desk, where the hands
were. The fingers opened bonelessly; they held the red
book as, in an olden portrait, a nobleman touches his watch
chain or rests his hand on a hound's silky ear. The nails
(Esther kept her own mitts, hot and sticky, in her lap) were
manicured and nothing sharp or bristled, or hard and hot or
rough, had savaged this skin. The hands were hairless, long-
fingered, and seemed to have an intelligence of their own.
Stop looking, Esther told herself, while the hexameters
were rippling from this god's pure lips.

Was he doing it, or was she? "Was it you who got this

started, or him?" Siri said, because now she was sitting up in bed with some color in her cheeks. "And answer. Don't think about it all day." Was it me or was it him? Was it something I said or did, or what I wore——. "Never mind," said Siri, but this was exactly what Esther wanted to think about——what had made it happen on this day instead of that. Siri solved this problem by saying that since it had happened, who cared? "Don't you remember when you came back here the first time and had to take a shower?"

Esther remembered. "He gave me something to read, and I read it."

"So?"

"I went back the next day, that day, you know, when you went to the infirmary."

"What day was that?"

"I don't know."

"Doesn't matter. So, you went back with the book. What was it?" Siri added: "Why am I asking? What do I care? Forget it."

"It was *Sir Gawain and the Green Knight*."

"What?"

"Never mind. It's not your field."

"Whose field is it?"

"Dr. Farrand's."

"Oh. Well, never mind. You read this green book and went back. So?"

"Let's skip over that. Nothing happened. He gave me another book. He was preparing his exam. You should see his writing. It could be in a museum. He uses an ink pen."

"So, you went home and read the second book?"

"I started a journal—not a day book, a journal. He asked me to. He calls it a 'commonplace' book, a book just for what you're reading."

"That makes me sick," Siri said, "but don't stop. It's got to get better."

This chattering chaff was making the good parts of the story evaporate. Esther said: "I'm going to the bathroom. I'll be back. Don't fall asleep." She used the walk and the time the way a monk would use his garden, for close-woven meditation.

Dr. Farrand read to me from *The Aeneid,* but I was too excited to hear a word. It was music with a slight New York accent. When he stopped and closed the book and looked—here was Sister. "Hello, Sister. Yes, better. She's resting."

When he looked at me, his eyes were a different color from what I thought—not black, but blue. (In the mirror, Esther saw her own sallow face with makeup smudged below her eyes. Was that what he was looking at? Couldn't be.) She splashed water on the face, using a paper towel to rub off the eye shadow. Who am I? she asked the reflection. Nothing but a big baby. But did that add to it?

No one would want to smooch with a baby. Smooch—what a word! The days were all stuck together like cards: what had happened on what day? And what was today? A weekend day, meaning Dr. Farrand was in his own home with his books and his groceries, and his drawers full of folded clothes. Was he neat?

It was too exciting.

"Don't tell yourself the story," Siri said, when Esther got back. "Tell me."

"I'm trying to."

"Well, try harder."

"Do you want to hear it from the beginning?"

"Yeah. I already know the end."

"You do?"

"But you don't."

"I don't?"

"Well, you don't want to hear it, but you know it, too."

"Shh. Don't spoil it."

It began fifty, sixty years ago, when Esther was still a freshman with baby fat. (Siri laughed: "You've still got it.") After reading whatever he read from *The Aeneid,* he was silent, not one peep out of him until I had to look to see if his eyes were open, or if I weren't suddenly by myself. ("Yeah?") He was looking at me. And there was nothing I could think of to say. What do I know after all? Nothing. I hadn't even read one medieval epic, long or short. ("As if that matters.") That's what you don't understand, Siri. It does matter. ("Wrong!") Time passed. After a while, I got used to it. We sat there just breathing. He was looking at me, and sometimes I looked, but most of the time, I read the spines of his books. After a while, he got up and opened a window to look out. He called me over to see what he was looking at. Miss Ferry, he called me. I got up and tried walking, but one foot was asleep. "See," he said, "you can see the moon and the sun in the same quarter of the sky." He put his hand on the back of my neck and pointed my head to where the moon was. "A young moon," he said. And I was thinking about that when someone knocked. It was the janitor. I ran out and he came in."

"A young moon," Siri said. "What did he mean?"

"I don't know. It's probably allegorical," Esther said. "Allegorical means it says what it says and then it says something else deeper."

"So that's all?"

Esther nodded.

"In three days?"

"The moon was today. The other days were different."

"It took *three days* for the moon to happen?"

"I skipped a day. I skipped a day after the first day."

"Why?"

Esther didn't know why. "So what's the end you're thinking you know?"

"There's still time to get out of it."

"To get out of what?"

"To get out and be free."

Esther considered. "Maybe so," Esther said. "But I don't understand why suddenly you know everything."

"I know things."

"Everybody knows something."

"Yes, but no one ever asks me what I know."

This struck Esther as funny. Siri had gone from not being able to think an abstract thought to seeing the future—or thinking she did. Esther decided to hold on, at least for now, to the unpredictability, the incommensurability of Dr. Farrand. It could be true. Siri was seeing a pigeonhole with a trapdoor, but Esther was seeing infinity.

Esther wondered if the talk had hurt the experience. The picture she had of Dr. Farrand was fading: there wasn't even a face above the dark jacket. The act of trying to remember was washing out the memory. Esther looked at

Siri, heaped up on the bumpy bed like a load of clean clothes. To think that so much had happened, and they were still freshmen.

"Are you asleep?" Esther said.

"No."

"Well, get up," Esther leapt up on the twin bed and began to jump. The springs were screaming. Esther fell to her knees and jumped back to her feet.

"Get off," said Siri, grinning.

"No, you get on!"

They both jumped, each on a bed, until Siri was choking for air. She sat with her head over her knees. "Open the window," she croaked.

5.

When the doctor came to give a booster shot on Monday morning, he said to Siri: "Young lady, be aware of the fact that you're not strong and when you don't bounce back—at your age—that's a bad sign. What I'm saying," he went on, sinking the needle into Siri's muscleless thigh, "is you need to build yourself up." He handed her a calorie chart and a booklet of Air Force exercises, and said he'd be back for a third shot that day.

Siri had only two classes and both met after lunch, so she could have built herself up by slopping around in robe and slippers until lunchtime, but she had other plans. First was to clean up, because the nuns didn't have a shower and she had gotten by on one sponge bath. Getting up and out of the room with an armful of shampoo, powder, towels, a razor and hand cream posed the first hurdle. When she arrived in the bathroom, she sunk to the floor in a miasma of sweat and vertigo. The floor was cold. Next step was to turn all the showers on to hot and heat the place up. Third was to get into one with the shampoo.

She was on the way (if she could but get out of the dorm dry and dressed) to see this Dr. Farrand she'd heard so much about. She knew what she thought of him, but wanted to see with her own eyes.

The hot shower was debilitating and an hour elapsed before Siri reached the top of the stairs and inched her way down, grabbing the handrail and panting. It took time to get down, but that she had lots of. The campus smelled strange, like a factory or a locker room. There was a rubbery, ashy smell and it wasn't spring because false spring had been beaten back and the earth looked gray, the sky was gray, and the sand used to bank the curving roadways—so graceful to look at, but so treacherous in winter—was blowing in circles. Siri felt a cold drop on her nose, but it was useless to hurry. She was permanently slowed, what with the leaden limbs and vertigo, and lungs barely open for business. Tying her scarf around her head (still wet), she trudged to the mailbox at the end of the sidewalk, touched its freezing blue flank, and turned around. Stooge! Dr. Farrand was in the basement. No need to go out at all.

Back inside, all was warmth and the stale odor from the convent. Siri pushed on. Down the steps and along the corridor, vacant with boot-smudged linoleum. Siri had only visited one office—the philosophy nun's, and she was in the library. Except for the mail room, she had never ventured down this corridor. Few girls did. She passed a block of closed doors with names pinned on cards. She didn't recognize any names, and, reaching the fire door, had to turn back, knowing that Esther had lied. Maybe the whole story was made up! But no, here he was. Since his door was open, Siri hadn't seen the name. Inside was nothing. She stood in the doorway. The room was no bigger than a closet, but the guy had covered the white walls with bookshelves and the linoleum—as Esther had said—with an Oriental rug. What

she hadn't said was the rug was too big and he had to double it up, so it was full of folds and wrinkles. No overhead
light and a curtain on the window, so the lamp with its red
shade made the room look like a fortune teller's. Siri spotted the ink pen and the little red books. (They must always
be on the desk, the faker!) He had a plant and Siri was on
her way to inspect it (was it real?) when, from behind, she
heard: "Excuse me?"

"What kind of plant is that?" she asked, without turning.
"Do you mind my asking?"

"No," he said, "but may I ask what you're doing in my
office? Shouldn't you be in class?"

"Is it real?" Siri went on, still facing away, composing
herself. This guy was not going to get the advantage of his
sudden appearance.

"Go ahead and see," the voice said. "Will you excuse
me?" He brushed past and settled himself at his desk. Siri
went to the plant and touched a leaf. It felt real, but so
what? How was she to know—in this dark cubbyhole?

"Would you like to sit down?" the man said. It was Dr.
Farrand. It had to be.

"Are you Dr. Farrand?" Siri said, still looking at the
plant.

"Yes. And you are?"

At least she had gotten that right. "I'm in the wrong
room, excuse me," said Siri. "I didn't mean to bother you."

She was now facing the corridor.

"Who were you looking for?"

Siri couldn't think of any faculty names, not even a nun's
name, and the nuns didn't have offices down here.

Since there was no dignified way to answer, or to leave, Siri sat down on the victim's chair. She had never been to an office hour, but grasped the symbolism of the arrangement.

"Are you all right? You look a little pale."

Siri took him in. Much younger than what Esther had said. Esther had made him sound Dad's age or older. Homely—well, that went without saying. His hair was black and curly, yet crispy, as if he never got it clean. It looked a little like fur. He wore wire-framed glasses and was thin—his shirt sunk in at the chest. Who did he look like? Eddie Fisher? Sal Mineo? This was no dreamboat. Did Esther think he was? He didn't even look like a normal American. That thought absorbed Siri for a minute. Meanwhile, Dr. Farrand had caught up: he was studying her!

"I'm not in English," Siri said, trying to catch up with him.

"Oh," he said.

"But my roommate is." Siri waited for him to ask for Esther's name, but he didn't. Did he know?

"What's your major, if you don't mind my asking?"

"I don't have one. I've been sick."

He nodded. Suddenly, Siri remembered all the pompous things he had said about who could be in English and who couldn't. Who did he think he was! (And now Esther was in his clutches.)

"I've got another student coming right before lunch," he said, looking at his watch. "What can I do for you—or, were you just looking around?"

Siri took a breath. These were painful because her lungs were clogged and sometimes a deep breath dislodged the gunk, and set off a round of coughing. She choked the beginning of one back, nipping it in time by quick (gross) swallows of phlegm.

Keep your bloody hands off my roommate, you piece of shit! she wanted to say, because she was still weak, and without Esther, might have to go home and stay home. Something held her back. All she did was stare. Into the stare she put it all. She was sure, when he blinked, that— plain as day—he'd gotten the message.

Or had he? "Miss?" he said, as she cleared the corner, "would you give this" (getting up to hand her a paperback) "to Esther Ferry? Do you know who she is?"

Like a robot, Siri nodded and took it.

"Tell her to come and see me. Tell her to put the other aside and start here."

"Okay," Siri said, still nodding on command. She heard the door close and then the eleven fifty bell went off and, in minutes, the corridor was flooded. Not here, where she was standing near the faculty offices, but there, where the mail room was, with bulletin boards for mixers and rides and weekends off campus, for spring break, summer jobs and junior year abroad. Siri summoned her energy and pro-pelled herself to the stairway, up one, up two, and to the lounge where no one went except during reading week. She found an overstuffed chair with a bed sheet on it and sank down. She sniffed the sheet and sneezed. The chair was dusty; the room was dusty and even this clean sheet some freshman with allergies had slapped down was dusty. Siri pinched her nose, but sneezed anyway, and kept sneezing until there was nothing left: snot or impulse. She fell back in the chair and closed her eyes. When she opened them, she saw the book was a thick one: *Romance of the Rose*.

She'd never heard of it. Opening it, she saw on a blank leaf some tiny writing: "To Timothy, Christmas Day, 1968, from Mother." Siri started to read. Soon she was asleep. When she woke up, cold and sneezing, it was late afternoon; the room was dark, but the campus floodlights striped the floor and ran up the chairs. This was scary and Siri pulled herself out of the slick-sheeted chair; there was something hard under her leg and it was the book. What book didn't matter. Nothing mattered but the fact that life had unraveled once again, and Siri felt lost, afraid, lonely, ready to cry and give up, but first she had to get to the bathroom and out of this haunted house, which was not just this lounge, not just Great Hall, but the whole leprous, devily place, a house of horrors. It was enough to make you scream.

Back in the infirmary, with orders to spend a week, in spite of the fact that she was better; hardly coughing at all, and the bit of green she choked up was from the last infection. The doctor was firm. Stay or go home. Siri asked for a pad and Monica went scurrying away three times before she came up with something Siri could write on.

"Dear Esther," she wrote. She didn't know the date, or even what day it was. Every day was cloudy through the dirty windows. Were they dirty? They were windows made out of glass cinderblocks, so there was no view and only a milky light. She summoned everything she had.

"You're my only friend," she wrote. "I could have more friends, and need to, but now I just have you. I was just starting to like college. If I saw you, I'd never admit this to your face, but I love it. In my whole life, I've never had such peace and quiet, with no one butting into my business, or blabbing at me all the livelong day. I can read if I want to, or talk to you, or you can talk to me. I'm never lonely, or I wasn't until now. All I'd like to do, all I'm asking is to go back to the life I had before Dr. Farrand got involved. I don't trust you with him, Esther. And I don't trust him with you. What you don't know is I met him and he gave me something to give you. I don't know where it is now. It's gone. He likes you, Esther. Even I could see that. And you like him. (That's an understatement.) But he's not right for you. You're a freshman in college, Esther, and he's too old. You're just a baby to him."

Siri was running out of words, but she still had more to say. She had to be careful not to sound like Sybele nagging. Better to sound like Dad giving easy-to-take advice, but his advice was useless. Live and let live—that was Dad's main advice, and what good would that do Esther? None. Because if she lived and let live, Dr. Farrand would have his chance.

"You're too young, Esther," Siri wrote. "You're even younger than I am. I can't come up—at least not right now—with all the arguments I need to convince you. It's partly your fault because you were supposed to teach me how to think, or was that what I was going to teach you? But you never did. Stay away from him, Esther. Or I'll tell your mother and father. And don't do anything till I get back."

When would she be back? It was useless asking Monica, the stupidest person she'd ever met. And the doctor wasn't making any promises. She had no credit with him, he said, because he couldn't trust her to take care of herself.

Siri signed her name, first and last. "P.S.," she wrote. "Come and see me. Soon!"

And Esther came, before she even could have gotten the letter, because Siri needed an envelope to send it and Monica was finding one for her. It was too late. One look at Esther's face and you could see that. She didn't even need to open her mouth.

Esther sat in Monica's chair. Instead of a matching skirt and sweater from Siri's closet, she had on a dungaree skirt and white shirt. No makeup and the hair as crazy as it had been when Siri first saw her. She looked like Little Orphan Annie. But it was still the same old Esther.

"You look like hell. What happened?"

"I got another cold. Did that Dr. Farrand guy tell you I came by?"

"What?"

"I went and saw him. He gave me something for you."

"*The Romance of the Rose?*"

"I don't know. Something."

"I have it. He gave it to me himself."

"He gave it to *me* to give you."

"Well, you didn't, did you?"

"I can't even remember, but I don't know how he got it back."

"Never mind. I have it. Thanks for trying to give it to me."

That reminded Siri of the unsent letter. "Esther," she said.

"Yeah?"

"I wrote you a letter from here."

"Yeah? Well, give it to me."

Siri found it on the bedside table. "Don't read it now. No, I changed my mind—read it."

Esther read. Siri watched her face. She was concentrating but all kinds of different looks flitted across her flat face. It was hard to separate them out, and none was pleasant.

"Thanks for this."

"Why are you thanking me?"

"I appreciate your concern."

"When you say that, I feel like your aunt or uncle."

"You know what I mean."

The exchanged petered out here, and no one wanted to restart it. It was too late. The damage was done.

"Is it?" Siri asked.

"Is it what?"

"Are you involved with that professor?"

Esther didn't answer. Why answer? What happened had happened. There were no words to put on it. She wasn't involved—and she was. "I'd still like to be friends. I need friends now," she said.

"True."

"Why should I not have friends because of him?"

"Him who?"

"You know who."

"You can't even say his name! That's how guilty you are."

But where was it all to lead? And how much going energy did it have? Esther was different. She looked as if she went to a public college in Boston. She stood out and the nuns were already ragging her for the dungaree skirt (not a real skirt to them; the marks of disrespect—tight and question-able fabric; the way it was fastened by a stud, a metal but-ton and an industrial zipper—were all over it). They didn't like the unironed white shirt either, oversized. No one but Siri knew where she'd gotten it (from him). Even Mr. Whitman noticed. During an office hour, he'd said: Esther Ferry, you're a different person. What in God's name has happened to you? He grinned when he said it, because he liked the change, although Esther didn't tell him who was responsible for it. Siri had said: don't tell anyone, and that seemed wise, but for Esther, it was the beginning of a sec-ond life, and the first time she'd hidden anything from any-one. Just the hiding had altered her appearance. Her face was less sarcastic-looking. You couldn't tell what she was thinking, but you could see that she *was* thinking. No one guessed.

One time Esther was in his car. They drove to Wellesley and had coffee at Brigham's. Siri was on pins and needles, but Esther was only gone a couple of hours. There was no way you could get married in that short a time, or get preg-nant, although she wasn't sure about the latter. It might take less time if you were sure of a place to do it. No one—not even Esther—was going to do it in broad daylight on a street in Wellesley, or even in a park. Besides, she told Siri (did Siri believe her?) there was nothing like that "between us." Siri didn't like the sound of "between us," as Esther put it. "Us" made them seem like equals, and he was still twenty or thirty years older, or at least ten—a good ten—and "between us" was too cozy. Those words coming so easily to Esther's lips were proof that something had already happened. She was no longer the old Esther, and not even the Esther she pretended to be. Siri saw it all, and thought it through (was this "thinking"?) in those two hours on the Sunday afternoon when Esther met Dr. Farrand half a mile from the campus entrance—there where Route 22 met the Highland Road, at the bus shelter, in case he was late. Those were her instructions.

Siri walked Esther to the campus gates. Esther had begged her to come—that's how nervous she was, but Siri could see that the nervousness was really something else, something better that no one but Esther was in on. This made Siri too irritated to walk even one step farther, and Esther seemed to understand. It was like death, Esther said.

"What's like death?"

"You have to do it alone," Esther said. "No one can come with you."

"He's going with you!" Siri said, but Esther had picked up speed and was halfway down the college walk, almost to the "open," where the houses began.

As Siri toiled up the hill, breathless because still recuperating, she tried to follow Esther in her mind, as the last minutes of freedom elapsed—except that wasn't what Esther would be thinking. Just the opposite, probably. She wasn't dragging her legs to stretch out the time, she was pounding along. (What shoes did she have on? Sneakers? Yes. Now Esther was wearing sneakers and no stockings— bare-legged on this chilly day—raining, windy and raw.)

Siri had to stop and sit on the wall. That's how out of breath she was, dizzy and perspiring from the effort. She was too fagged now to think, but in her mind's eye, Esther was still pounding away toward that bus stop. Siri could even see the car parked with the motor running, and Esther galloping at top speed to jump in. Siri thought her heart might stop, but a minute later, she was on her feet, laboring up the hill. She wondered if her thinking alone was keeping Esther alive. Keep going, she told herself, even though it's killing you.

A thought shot through Siri's mind as she rested on the ground floor, before taking the steps: this was Sunday, but Sunday had changed. How had it changed so much? It was not the Sunday of high school or, even worse, a child's endless, boring Sunday. Sunday was now a living day, full of prospects like the one Esther was delving into. Sunday was date day and there was something gorgeous about it, if it would only happen to someone else.

If I don't concentrate, Siri reminded herself upon reaching the second landing, Esther's a goner. Siri tackled the third and fourth staircases like an athlete in training, pacing herself, breathing before each fourth step, and holding that breath, forcing it down to where the lungs were still soggy. When she arrived, grasping the bannister, she almost rocked backwards, so dizzy from the effort. Lifting one leaden leg, then another, sliding the smooth soles of the well-worn flats along the slippery linoleum, she was there, flung open the door, slammed it shut, and dove onto the bed, hanging onto its sides, even laughing a little in excitement.

Lack of oxygen gave Siri's head movie of Esther a lurid

cast—there were reds and blacks, plus purple floaters, some of the best afterimages she'd ever seen.

In their intensity, Siri had forgotten what Farrand looked like, so she substituted the actor in the French movie *A Man and a Woman*. Now Esther was in a racing car and the object was not a sundae at Brigham's.

In real time, Esther was still in the bus shelter with a cleaning lady coming back after the weekend. At first, Esther didn't want to talk to her, but she could be her own mother! The lady commented on the sneakers with no socks. From that detail—and no coat—she deduced that Esther was a college girl from that local college. Where was she going? There was no bus service on Sunday.

Luckily, the housekeeper was picked up first, by a station wagon full of brats. The housekeeper climbed in back and one of the kids sat on her lap. The housekeeper waved the child's hand at Esther. Right behind the wagon was a junker. It can't be, Esther thought, but it was. An ancient sedan, Chevy or Ford, with all the trim pulled off, and a cheap paint job, chocolate brown. Inside was Dr. Farrand. Esther could see him through the windshield. She knew she was supposed to hustle into the front seat, but her legs were glued to the wooden bench of the bus shelter. In that one glance, what was between them dissolved. They stared through the thick glass with a few wet leaves stuck to it. Neither could turn that moment into the next. The embarrassment was too great. A few cars passed, slowed to look. Esther knew she had to get up. Life never stopped dead until death stopped it, and this wasn't that. She stood, her pocketbook (a knitted envelope with a long cord strap) fell to the ground and the few things in it fanned out on the dirt. By then, Dr. Farrand was out of his car, but just standing there. Esther leaned over to swipe the objects (handkerchief, lipstick, gum, penknife, glasses) back into the bag's open mouth and lifted it by the cord. Dr. Farrand approached. "Hi," he said, and his nervousness pushed two or three wavering syllables into the greeting.

"Hi," Esther said back, and that was done.

"Where are we going?" he asked, taking her by the elbow, as if she were old and ailing, and guiding her toward the door. When Dr. Farrand had gotten in and closed his door and adjusted his rearview mirror and unlocked the emergency brake, he sat there with the motor running. "Are you okay?" he asked.

Esther was feeling better. The car smelled of pipe tobacco and the backseat was full of books, proving he *was* a professor and not some grease monkey picking up a girl at the bus stop. Esther wanted to ask an intelligent question, but none came to mind. Maybe it was up to him to provide the conversation. Everything about this "date" was off. Outside of his cubby of an office, the world was big and shapeless, and looked just like everyone else's world. By comparison, St. M's now seemed exotic with its corridorful of nuns and ranks of collegians in matching sweaters and skirts. Esther herself was a damp, shivering mess: wrinkled skirt, red hands and a big lump of a pocketbook. How had things gotten so far?

"How are you today?" Dr. Farrand was asking, patting Esther's bare knee.

"Fine, and you?"

"Did you have a plan?"

"I thought," Esther said, and heard her own matter-of-fact tone, "you wanted to have coffee."

"Did I?" he said, scratching his head.

Esther put on her glasses and felt better. Dr. Farrand's lower half was in blue jeans with black wingtips. His upper half was a loose, zipped jacket. Why had she been thinking there was something wrong with him? That they might be two of a kind—losers, as Siri would be quick to say if she saw them at the bus stop, or clunking along in this beat-up car, aging like a downtown bus. That thought made Esther laugh and already she was feeling lots better, more like her old self, before this annihilating crush had hit her.

Three cups of coffee into the afternoon and Dr. Farrand was talking up a storm. He had outlined the chapters of his dissertation, accepted for publication if he could shave it of two to three hundred pages. "That's a lot," Esther said, and he agreed. Each sentence had cost him. He'd been working on it for the past ten years, doing all this dog work to support life after his department had cut him off from funding.

Esther asked what dog work, but before a word was out of his mouth, she knew it was teaching at the all girls St. M's, where there was no graduate program and just a handful of majors. "A waste of precious time," he was saying.

"What about you? How's your work going?" he said, when the waitress dropped the check on the tabletop. He dug out his wallet and found a two-dollar bill to pay for all that coffee. The place was closing. The cash registers were already emptied.

"I guess we should go," he said.

Esther was relieved. She'd only written two term papers, and both had gotten As, but they were only fifteen pages long, including the bibliography and footnotes. All she'd taken so far was survey courses. She didn't even own her own books. What work had she done that Dr. Farrand could possibly care about?

The thought sank Esther, and even the two kisses that Dr. Farrand ("Tim, Tim!" he'd said, but in her mind he was still Dr. Farrand) gave her didn't cheer her up. She didn't even feel them. "You're a beautiful girl," he said, and although it sounded nice, it wasn't true. He was too old for her and too smart.

"Goodbye for now," he said, stopping at the bus shelter, even though it was dark and no one would see if he'd driven her closer—say, to the college gate. "I can't wait till Monday."

"What's Monday?" Esther asked.

"That's when I'll see you again."

It was dark and there were no streetlights, only the light from inside the houses, and freezing cold. Esther's feet were soaked and one shoe caught in a tree root. There was no real sidewalk. She made it, finally, to St. M's stone wall, with walkway and lights, and although a quarter of a mile long, Esther was almost home.

Siri could tell something was different, and so different, it was safe now to put the whole chapter behind them. Esther was no more in love than she herself was, when she thought of Christo, or the babies who'd preceded him. Siri wanted to laugh and enjoy this to the full, but Esther was still in a delicate state. How did she know? Well, one thing: she was crying.

Siri let her cry it out. She was a cryer and it wouldn't hurt to face up to her stupidity, as Siri had to all the time, ever since coming to college, although she was no cryer. It was back to work, she wanted to tell Esther—and did tell her—but it didn't do any good. Work—just the word—made Esther cry harder, and say, "What work do *we* have?"

Siri was shocked. Had this changed her that much? Was their life different now, after Siri had put so much into loving college and the strange work that came with it? If so, then Esther was no friend, and all this time had been wasted.

Siri wanted to kill Esther, pull her hair and scratch her face, but Esther was still crying, so instead of attacking, Siri took out the electric (which she hadn't yet touched, much less used) and found a piece of onionskin.

"Dear Esther," she typed, with two fingers.

Just writing these words made her feel better. Writing "Esther" and "Dear" gave a certain command of Esther and of the situation—whatever had happened on the date, which Siri still didn't know. Meanwhile, Esther stopped crying and was standing behind her, reading what she hadn't yet written.

"What?" Esther said. "What?"

"Go to hell," Siri was tempted to type because she was angry that Esther had had an adventure, however awful, and Siri hadn't. But that's the kind of thing you didn't have to write because you could say it faster, let it be heard and forgotten. That's what speech was. Writing it was different. Siri was a thinker, but not a writer.

Esther was waiting, and, guessing that Siri didn't know what to say, she eased her off the chair and sat on it herself.

"Dear Siri," she typed under "Dear Esther." "Don't think I don't understand what you're trying to tell me, even if you don't have the words for it."

Siri waited to read what it was she intended to say. She'd recognize it, even if she couldn't say it just now.

"You were right, and you are right," Esther typed. "What did Heraclitus say? 'A fool is excited by every word.'"

Siri laughed, when she saw that one come out. Did that sentence apply? If it did, she didn't see how. And then, the next sentence rolled out of the machine: "'What do we mean by fool?"

Esther looked at Siri and they screamed it out: "We think we know what is meant by fool, and maybe we do."

Later, when they were both in bed, Esther told the story. To Siri's ears, it was a thousand times worse and more disgusting than Esther could even imagine. Dr. Farrand was a loser, and did Esther want to make things worse for herself by association? It was easier to slip down than to climb up. Esther corrected Siri. She didn't really understand, although she had grasped the social dynamics, perhaps even the class dynamics. (Siri was proud of this twofold grasp, and was waiting to hear what she didn't know). Dr. Farrand, didn't she see, had written a book. He was a doctor, and Esther was a freshman, an A student, yes, but a freshman.

Siri didn't like the sound of this because she, too, was a freshman. Esther said: No, you're not even there yet. You're on probation.

Next thing, Esther was asleep. She hadn't slept much the night before. Siri was awake. She was still composing a letter. Esther had written back before Siri could even finish saying what she had to say. That was unfair, and so was saying that Esther was a real freshman and Siri wasn't. It was unfair, but it was true. Siri could feel herself dividing: one part knew it was unfair and the new part knew it wasn't. Siri, according to the new part, hadn't earned any college credits. No, that was an overstatement. She had earned three full credits for the C in history. She had taken one college course and passed it. Would she ever enroll in another, and also pass it? Being sick had eaten away hours of class time in College English and History of the World, Part 2. She might as well drop history, but College English was still an option. This course involved writing and just the other day, Monica had told her she was a natural storyteller. (Monica meant liar, but the nun was kind enough to say "storyteller," and to say it in a pleasant tone.)

Siri got up and turned her desk lamp on. What a nice cone of light it made, and some of it fell on the desk. All this time, she could have used this lamp. It was just a cheap thing, but in the dorm room, it made as good a light as the expensive brass lamps at home. What was in a lightbulb? She had never taken physics, where light was studied. All she knew was it took a plug and a switch and the filament glowed in a frosty or see-through glass. How wonderful it was to have just enough of it for yourself, but no more. The floor and ceiling were dark, and a tent of thick darkness blocked Esther's bed from sight.

Siri knew enough not to type, even on the electric. She took a sheet of filler paper and started the letter over. On the page, she wrote the story of Esther's date. The way it should have happened.

"Dear Esther," she wrote in a hand that looked childish, big and erratic, but go on, she said, go on. Dear Esther. "Tonight, you had your first date." (Was it her first date? Who knew, who cared? This was writing, not eyewitness.) "And everything went wrong that could go wrong, except you came back in one piece, still alive. I've had a lot more dates than you, but I could say the same thing. Everything goes wrong. When will that ever stop?"

Siri crossed out this paragraph, but left the "Dear Esther."

First paragraph, fresh page. "Here's how it should have gone. When my dad met my mom, he was in a fraternity of all men. Dad played sports, but I forget which one. Maybe sailing or football. He was tall and handsome and I'm not just saying that because he's related. He still is, and you've seen him with your own eyes. He was at Harvard University, which you know, because you've seen his Harvard ring, which I have. He met my mother exactly the way you met the creep who took you to Wellesley on a big date, and left you on the side of the road. He was coaching girls here in sailing, so it must have been sailing that was his sport. I don't know. He took girls like my mother to Lake Cochituit, somewhere out in the country. That's how they met."

Siri's hand hurt from clutching the pen and pressing so

hard. The letter was already too long, and maybe none of this was any of Esther's business. But that thought broke the mood, and suddenly Siri could hear Esther's snaggly breathing, so better to go back to the writing and think about Dad and Sybele—putting her own self in Sybele's place. See if that worked, and if it did—

"Dad came out to Weston—where we are—once a week to take these girls to Lake Cochituit. One day a storm came up and Sybele had a cold, maybe a fever (because she was always sick, like me). Dad had to rescue her sailboat, which tipped over so the sails got wet and dragged the whole thing down. Sybele couldn't really swim; she said she could to get into the class, but she still can't."

Now her hand was crippled from the effort. It was hard to uncurl the fingers.

"Dad got both girls into his boat and carried my mother up to his car. She was hysterical. And—now I remember—she had the flu and was sick as a dog, but went sailing that day because it was the last class of the year and she might never see Dad again. 'Mr. Sorenson,' they had to call him, even though he was only a few years older."

Was that it? Siri knew the rest of it, but didn't like to think about it. Aunt Bay had told her, or she'd heard it when Aunt Bay was telling a grown-up. "You couldn't have been that sick," Bay said to Sybele. Dad thought it was funny, but Sybele didn't. For Sybele, it wasn't a nice story. She got Dad, true, and got pregnant with a baby, Siri, true, but the way it happened—so hilarious to Bay and Duke and even Dad—was not funny at all to Sybele.

Siri wanted Esther to wake up so she could tell her this

story instead of having to write every word. She still didn't get the story and Esther might. The facts did not make a picture that Siri could accept as true or realistic. Maybe it was because it happened in the old days, when things were all in black and white, like the mishmash of family photos in the album.

Siri's own past didn't add up, so how could she put this incident, Dad and Mom's first date—when she wasn't even there to see and no one thought to give her a full version of it—into a picture that would convince Esther that this was a date, and she hadn't had one yet? Dad and Mom's date, sickening though it was to contemplate, was real. After Dad carried Mom to the car (Siri didn't know what kind, but Dad had cool cars with all their chrome and no cheap paint jobs), she got a little better, especially after they dropped the other girl off and drank some restorative scotch or whiskey, which Dad kept in the trunk for emergencies, and peeled off her gym suit and put on one of Dad's sweatshirts and his suede jacket. (Siri had seen pictures of this jacket.)

So Sybele was dried off, and had a few sips of whiskey, and off they drove to Harvard Square, because Dad couldn't drop Sybele at college, sick and cold and half drowned. How sick was she? Siri wondered. Maybe not sick at all. Could she swim? She said she couldn't, but Siri remembered her swimming out to the raft on Waterman's Lake. Did that change the story?

Was Dad the kind of guy—fast—to sneak Sybele into his room, with his roommates—or "suitemates," as he called them? Was Mom the kind of girl—dumb—to do it on the first date? They went through the basement of the

"house"—Dad called it a house, but it was a brick dormi-
tory like all the rest. Why did she go along with it?

Siri put down the pen—the letter could be finished any-
time—and flopped on her bed. Mom was pretty, yes. (In
this story, it was hard to use the sarcastic tone that went
with the word "Sybele.") She was, although her legs were
thick. Dad said he liked legs to be thick, and not to diet
them down to twigs. (Were Siri's legs twigs?) She was just
a kid when he'd said that, so it didn't matter. Mom was
almost as tall as Dad, an armful, Dad liked to say, with
"plenty of brisket," as he put it, "fore and aft." Sybele hated
to hear this, but also liked it, because her face turned red
and almost black if she were in a bad mood. It was funny to
see this.

Siri had not done it, or come anywhere near. Christo
was too much of a baby and the thugs she'd met so far at
mixers would never talk her into going all the way with the
likes of them. They could force her, sure, but she'd never
give them the chance. She wasn't like Sybele, desperate for
attention and ready to give in to anyone who liked her.

Esther wasn't exactly like this. Why, then, was Esther so
far out on a limb? Was dating that important to her? It was
important to Sybele, because it was the only thing she had.
It was her whole life, finding someone like Dad, and landing him. A good "provider," as Siri heard him described by
Sybele's friends, to show what Dad had to offer when
Sybele was complaining about what he didn't have.

PART TWO

6.

Esther was enrolled in a music course—appreciation and
history. The library had one listening room, which also
functioned as a storage room for film, photos and the few
rare books the library owned. The class was small—fifteen
students—almost all music majors with their own record
players, so Esther had the listening room to herself. She
used it for studying, not just for listening. It was a respite
from Siri and her rants. In two years, Siri had become a
marathon talker, interested in every thread of thought,
every nugget of wisdom gleaned from books, or from the
odd experience to be had on the isolated campus with no
friends but Esther, and the few resident professors she
could pin down in their office hours. Esther needed some
peace, and the cramped closet with the turntable and the
beat-up speakers offered that and more.

Music was an elective and nothing in Esther's busy past
offered a clue to how it was to be received, criticized or
even remembered. The course material was chronological,
and luckily, Esther had heard Gregorian chant in the occa-
sional High Mass—not at her dinky church, but at the
cathedral. Parochial school children learned how to sing
plain chant, and to read it, but it was the men and boys who
filled the choirs and sang with an organ note for pitch. The

course began with chant in the Age of Gregory and Charlemagne, and the textbook contained illuminated pages from
codexes and hourbooks. The text was useful, and it could
be read, but music, as everyone knew, was not something
for the eyes.

Esther had always liked music, but the Ferrys didn't, and
their floor-model radio was as often on the blink as not, and
staticky at best. It stood in the den where the TV set was, so
usable only when Anna wasn't watching her daytime "stories" or Daddy, boxing matches and bowling games, west-
erns and game shows, which he loved and played so loud it
was hard to read let alone listen to music. Esther got a plastic transistor radio for her sixteenth birthday, but it only
played the AM band. Sometimes, late at night, a local station featured jazz or blues; otherwise the music was "Hit
Parade" standards sung by Patti Page or Vic Damone.

Esther used the radio to keep up with the Beatles and the
Rolling Stones, since she was never going to own any of
their records, and to be alive and under twenty, you had to
know the up-to-the-minute discography. This job was getting harder as the bands multiplied. It was mostly a boy
thing, but a mistake to fall too far behind. One listen was
enough for Esther, whose brain was like flypaper.

This ability did not translate into the realm of classical
music in the "common practice" period. Listening to this
music was like dreaming and thinking rolled into one, only
it wasn't just you; it was the musician, the composer and
you working on the same thought, only they were always
ahead. Just as they were finishing, you were grasping the
arc's launch. And there were no words, of course, although

the knottiness of the texture felt like an argument, or like a long story, a fight or an elastically prolonged love scene. The teacher had warned them not to turn the pieces into movie music "for the head." It was not there for them to color in a trivial fantasy. And what were their fantasies, he said, if not naive, banal? The teacher was a hard nut; a former mathematician, he had worked on the Manhattan Project and, after a breakdown, had completely retooled. Esther liked him. Learning, like good house cleaning, required a stiff brush, an abrasive agent and a willing surface. Siri said that this sounded like fascist cant, but Esther reminded her of how much the housework "trope" had helped her, a total wipeout, become in two years an A student.

Siri was quick—quicker—but this kind of comment, or any reference to the "antediluvian" past, slowed her down, sometimes to torpor, and Esther—who feared a recurrence of what they had worked so hard to put behind them—changed the subject. But torpor was good, Siri insisted: the real head work got done in a torpid state. Was she right? Siri's torpor was quiet, yet the subcutaneous tension ionized the air. It was a good working condition, but it was the exception. Constant palaver in the small bedroom was the rule. Siri could not chew the tough meat of philosophical thought without talk. Talk was teeth and saliva. It chunked thought down to size. Esther understood, but it still ate too much time. There was no time for anything else, because Siri wanted to talk about her daily classes and the "Jamesian" experiences she was having with her teachers. She called them "stimulants" and "soporifics," but they were people, too, which is what made it Jamesian. While an English major for a month, Siri had taken a novel course and had encountered therein "himself," the one who could escort her, like Beatrice did Dante, to the higher realms. "What was that first guy's name," she asked Esther, "the one who took Dante up the first half?"

"Down," Esther said, "he took him down. Virgil."

"What's his whole name?"

Esther reached for the red volumes, which the roommates now owned. "Publius Virgilius Maro," she said, flipping to the first page.

"That's you. Esther Ferrius Maro."

The new, smart Siri was still the same bone-thin wreck she'd been when dumb, but there was something different about the way she walked and bore down on people—stimulants, soporifics, students, nuns, boys at mixers. The heart and guts of the thinking were done with Esther, who'd been her trainer and catalyst, no matter how tired she felt now, or how "depleted" (as Esther put it, still testing the girl's vocabulary) by the process. It was her responsibility. But other people (the stims and the sops) were necessary for growth, for pocket thought, parentheses, sidebars, test balloons.

Thank God, thought Esther, opening the door to the listening room, that she's still interested in "other people." The room was always unlocked, but you had to check out the albums, placed on reserve by Prof. Edelman. They were 78s from the RCA world-music library, a set of thick and bulky black disks. Their cardboard sleeves were so old, they crumbled at the touch. No liner notes. Even the center label was covered over. The records were numbered, so at least you could listen to the movements in their right order, but the listening was supposed to be context-free. Prof. Edelman had passed out notebooks with pages numbered to match the records. Student would identify the piece, the composer, the date, and make their comments. The music students found the "mystery" laughable: as if it took brains to separate out a Mozart from a Haydn, or a Bach from a Buxtehude. But for Esther, it was hard. All the music sounded good—as good as a 78 could sound on a iffy hifi filled with vacuum tubes. The smoke from the old-fashioned amp created its own TV-and-radio-shop humors, reminding Esther of *Sing Along with Mitch.*

But out of this stinky system came hyperpatterned sound, figures in the air of three and sometimes four dimensions. Esther felt the musical object lock onto her brain—a good fit. It was impossible to have an overview, the way you could in reading, if you simply stopped, slipped in a bookmark and veered off on your own line. You could stop the record, lift the needle—and you were supposed to do that—but the majestic body and wings of the musical beast dissolved in an instant. It was there, and advancing toward you, or not there at all. So, Esther left the needle down until it reached the paper disk, the end of the grooves. Often the piece continued on the flip side. There was so much of it! An endless stream. Prof. Edelman wanted the non–music major to get it all in order, to heap it into stylistic stacks, to identify signature phrases, or harmonic progressions of each composer. What was it like? It was like organizing beach sand.

But it was doable if you didn't try too hard. A lot of lazy listenings and, before long, the different animals emerged from the jungle, and then it was a mere matter of labeling the cages. The names were already there: Renaissance, classical, baroque, romantic, neoclassical, impressionist, folkloric, atonal. Once music had its place—pegs and holes—would it be the same? That was the kind of question that Siri could tackle because she still remembered prehistory, the diluvium of absolute ignorance, but Esther wanted to tackle it herself, now that she was a test case, and had a before, a now and maybe even an after.

Siri had shown her how to test this elemental reality because she had sharpened herself on the boundary line. She was hovering over both sides and could offer a view of the two fields and the division. It would not last. Time would rub away the division, the knifelike edge between ignorance and awareness. It would all run together—a continuous field of relativity—as it did for most people.

Esther had this one chance because music was a universe complete, and her ignorance total, although bit by bit, that perfect, blank globe was cut and scratched. Could these pinpricks and wrinkles be smoothed over? Esther closed her eyes, and there it was, at a little distance: the beginning, a round emptiness.

Was sound a swarm? Not when it came from these numbered 78s. Unit divisions were pressed into music. That was its defect, its limitation. It was composed with numeration in it, and not just the mathematical arts of harmony.

Even to the dunce, music presented itself in a line: beginning and ending, first, second and third. It was organized as other things were organized: three "squares," twenty-four hours, four seasons, plant, animal and mineral, male and female, space and object. Were these divisions real or factitious? Had someone done the numbers wrong, imposed divisions where none were natural?

Esther's head was whirling, or was it the effect of the needle lapping again and again on the cusp of the record label? What had she been listening to? Sibelius, the composer par excellence of the borderless.

By day, Esther was becoming glum and glummer. Siri antic and more. Siri was taking in all the world's knowledge in gulps, Esther letting it all out, a meditation on loss and emptiness. It was just an experiment, but the humors—those vultures, those vampires—always followed.

Dr. Farrand was begging Esther to go out with him. He didn't understand why she resisted setting a date. They could do anything: dinner, a film, a concert in Boston. Didn't she want to get out of this penitentiary? She did (or so she told him), and she liked him (she told him that, too), but she was not setting foot off campus until the mental unraveling stopped, or at least slowed down. So she told him she had too much work; her parents were coming to visit, or Siri's parents, or Siri was sick again—whatever came to mind. Soon, she was not welcome in his office, and then, her grade started to drop. She knew the answers to the quizzes—she still did all the reading—but she refused to supply these answers on demand. "Why?" Siri asked her. "Why do you see it as a demand? It's a requirement that you

read and spill. That's what you told me. Are you going back
on it now—just because it's him and you don't want to 'put
out'?

"Yeah," Siri said, in her new, authoritative voice. "Yeah,
that's what it is."

Esther wanted to protect her mind and its contents. She
had just enough in there. More—and she'd turn into Dr.
Farrand. Her head was filled, and now she needed to brood
over what she'd collected, and thin it out, if necessary. She
refused to be a container, a jug for teachers to fill, and then
empty. For at least a while, what was in there was all hers.
Would she organize it like a piece of music, like a story, or
just carve out entries and alphabetize them? Or just leave it
as it was, a mishmash? Compared to college, grammar
school was a Golden Age, where one thing built upon
another, and everything could be fit into its own box. Why
was that? Elementary knowledge was so well cooked that
even an idiot—and some of the grammar nuns surely
were—could make of it a tasty little feed: hotdog, roll,
Kool-Aid, Oreo. Had knowledge, rampant and unchecked,
gone wrong? Two forces alone kept it contained: if it were
useful to man or to God. Useful to man were arithmetic,
simple spelling and enough grammar to write a bread-and-
butter letter, enough natural history to recognize what was
in the world; golden rule, enough crafts to get through a
hot, boring summer; God knowledge was more extensive,
but at least focused on one thing, whether real or not. The
rest—and this was *all* of college—was knowledge for its
own sake. A bad bargain and one that had hidden costs.
Knowledge had a subtle economy, a devilish one. And what

had she done to poor Siri? Siri was Frankenstein's monster, although the poor thing thought she was Dante touring the three zones of the universe, each with a different, protective and masterful guide.

Esther had wronged Siri. This she thought sitting in the listening room as the record went round and the needle thumped against the paper disk. How long would it spin? Electricity powering the motor would persist, but the machine parts had a finite life—the short life of vacuum tubes and movable parts. Which would go first? The needle would wear away, or perhaps the paper would tear. The ultimate knowledge—the reward for the effort—was, Esther thought, the knowledge that everything was dying at its own rate.

Esther went to the listening room every day. Sometimes she listened to music, but always there came a point when the needle jogged out of its ultimate groove and starting whisking the paper disk. If Esther let the needle touch the paper, she left it there to revisit the only worthwhile knowledge: that everything was dying and dying at its own rate.

After a week of watching her roommate leave the dorm after lunch with no books, no pocketbook, no library card, and return hours later, dull, fagged, mute and sluglike, Siri decided to take action.

First, she had to find Esther. Not in the library—Siri searched every floor, table, nook and carrel. She even whipped through the stacks. She checked out the coffee shop and the dim conference rooms in the union. Not in the chapel either, but that was no surprise. Siri was not (no way!) going to walk the hills and dales and curving roads of the campus—that was going entirely too far, so she returned to the room.

There was a strange stillness that Siri had never noticed. Before, the empty room was filled with the clash of ideas, the inhalation of texts, the pounding of the heart as groaning heaps of intellectual matter were stacked and kicked over. The brain's normal workings were noisy, deafening at times. You could be lost in an instant, as thought scrambled over hedges and into the woods, or buried itself in a deep closet. You were never alone with brain work; it was never quiet like this. Siri listened until the room's small sounds bit into the solid cube of silence. Where the hell was Esther?

And meanwhile, Esther had broken through to the other side. And that side was a man's voice saying the listener had reached the end of RCA's library of classics, volume 14, disk 410. Esther lifted up her head from where it was resting on her folded arms. She had listened to the whole library. She could now stop. She had arrived at the end. The last vinyl platter had spun, and the urgings and longings evoked by its strange, coded message ceased to worm in and out. The cap was on and contents were sealed; these vinyls went back into their sleeves and cardboard cases, like a genie in its bottle. The agitation ceased, but it was different now inside and outside. The music had worked its magic. Esther felt she had lived many lives and all now buried, sucked into the ground. They were there, the lives, but unaccountable as forgotten dreams.

Esther returned volume 14, all twenty disks. She walked home in the dark. Her footsteps were rhythmic, as were the pulsing of the sodium lamps and the buzz of the generators. She found Siri sitting on the twin bed with vacant eyes and slack face that Esther hadn't seen since freshman year. She remembered it as the first in a series of stills—between this dullness and Siri's maddened élan were thousands of such stills, each one reflecting a stage in the quickening.

Siri and Esther were both now ready for life. The dross was burned and the soul laid bare.

Siri knew what she needed to know, and even more. There was extra, but not yet overmuch. She remembered everything she read. Once the light had turned on, she never thought to turn it off, to rest her eyes, to cool the lightbulb. On was on, and it was great—so different from off. Off was cold mud with rain dropping on it and night falling. On was a clean lab table with a 500-watt bulb, hot and hotter. Siri's hands were red and sweaty; the fingers were swollen, the nails bitten. She herself radiated heat. "I am so alive," she said to Esther. "I can hardly stand it. How can you stand it?"

Esther laughed. Siri had just reeled off two Shakespeare sonnets, memorized on the track, where she was sent to walk or run ten laps, morning and afternoon, as a substitute for the detested "team sports."

"Slow down," Esther said. "Listen to what you're saying. Otherwise, how is Shakespeare going to do you any good?"

But Siri couldn't slow down, and wouldn't. Speed was speed. Rather than slow down like the middle-of-the-road Esther Ferry, why not memorize all ninety sonnets, two at a time. How long would it take? Imagine what she'd have in her head. Something for any occasion. It didn't matter that Esther said dropping a line of Shakespeare into a bull session wasn't the thing in 1971. Vonnegut, Barthelme, Milo Minderbinder, Dr. Laing, George Gurdjieff or Ram Dass, but Shakespeare: no. No one would get it or like it.

Siri had nothing but contempt for these latecomers, the dross of the times. The modern—let alone the postwar or contemporary—had no interest for her. Everything had broken down after the French Revolution; and, for that matter, the Renaissance was a shadow, a hiccup, compared to its great original, and the Enlightenment, just a bland rehash of Plato and Aristotle, by less than stellar minds.

Esther loved hearing Siri slash away at history's monumental egos and pompous outworks. "Go to it, Sear!" she'd say, in spite of the fact that the music course, and the depression following, had drawn Esther into the mystics, where she met the zeitgeist eye to eye. It wasn't so bad, really. It was a way of being young, and Esther had never been young. Siri, on the other hand, had jumped from age ten to sixty in a few years' time. She was a hard-hat, Apollonian, elitist, a reactionary. Her ideas of reality were straight, uncut from *The Republic*.

How had she gotten so strong? No, Siri would have insisted, if she could hear the question: how have *you* gotten so weak?

It was a good question, although one Esther preferred to

consider alone. Of course, was it "weak" or was it tender? Was it tender or was it youthful? Was it youthful or romantic? Whatever it was, Esther was going with the tide.

She was the Dionysian; and, to Siri, this was noxious, but they were still roommates. Siri was having a wonderful year; Esther was still crawling around like a millipede. She had the legs to travel upside down on the ceiling, but chose to creep under the springs of the industrial-strength beds. They were juniors. Boston, their magnet city, was awash with youth, mostly of the Dionysian pattern, and the roommates explored the city together, returning by subway early, to meet the curfew and the last transport from Watertown station to the campus. To Siri, Boston was mostly the stores: Filene's and Lord & Taylor, Bonwit's, Peck & Peck and Best. As free agents, they trolled the aisles and rode the escalators. They watched the colors change from season to season, but fashion was going in one direction and the youth of Boston in another. Esther could feel it, but Siri saw nothing in either. The Boston Public Library was a very fine structure, as was the Richardson church, and it might have been worthwhile to be a Bostonian then, when that style gave the law, but the pointed fingers and tongues of modern buildings—International Style knockoffs—were silly, boring and sterile. They were not proper settings for the life of the mind.

Esther loved the parks—the grass, the statues and the swanboats. Yes, yes, said Siri, fine, so they'd go there in fine weather and into the North End for Italian food and street life. Touring was fun and every Saturday—when Esther could drag Siri away from Gibbon and Macauley—

they did it. Siri did it for Esther, who needed a break from brooding. Siri had watched all the energy drain out of "the Waltham girl," as she called her, to prick her from these doldrums. Walking the streets woke her up. She even talked a little.

What she said was she was thinking of dropping out. Siri halted on the sidewalk. "Ferry, you stupid ass," she said. "This is your life."

"I don't care."

Esther was still walking and Siri had barely heard her answer.

They were on Newbury Street, a bright Saturday morning. Siri leaned against plate glass and cooled her forehead. It was a cafe window and people just inside stared at the hovering form to determine the meaning of this landing. The cool surface calmed a racing mind. Siri left her head there, but rolled it so the glass touched the right temple, then the left.

Esther had walked to the intersectiion. Was loneliness increased by singling out, by tapping the sidewalk with two feet instead of four? When the light changed, Esther looked at the row of cars ready to pounce. What if she forced them to stop? Would they? That kind of demonstration was empty, no matter how it panned out. "My cortex is still functioning," she whispered, recognizing the anti-senti-mental note. "Here I go," she said, stepping out, after the car flood had passed. "This is my first real step out of the dream."

"Esther!" she heard and turned. And there was Siri, falling into a storefront window, in slow motion.

"But why," Siri asked, when they had sat down in the cafe, "are you at a dead end?" Not waiting for an answer, she continued: "Dead ends can mean so many different things. It's a modern-day dodge. Can you support it with anything?"

"I don't want to discuss dead ends. Not right now. Okay?"

"But when you say something like that, you can't ignore your own words. Inside your own words is the key, Esther, to the mistake, the illogic."

"I'm dropping out."

"Same thing," said Siri. "Same damn thing. Examine your words. There is no 'out' to drop into. What are you going to do—be a waitress?"

"I don't care what I do."

They were drinking Earl Grey tea, loose in a porcelain pot with honey or sugar, or brown sugar or sweetener; with lemon, milk, cream or nothing at all to put in it. The scent alone savored of the ancient spice routes. Siri inhaled the steam and Esther stirred milk, cream, sugar and honey into her cup.

"Well, go then."

"I am going."

"What are you waiting for?"

"Don't rush me."

"Well, drink your tea then. Drink it and don't do anything rash."

"I need a fresh cup now."

"Why?"

"I put too much stuff into this one."

"Why did you?"

"I was testing the saturation of a solute."

Siri looked at the tea. "You can't do that experiment if you put cream in it."

"How do you know?"

"I read it somewhere. Trust me. I know."

Fresh cups were brought and a new pot.

"You feel better now, don't you?" Siri said, after they'd each had a cup.

"I don't know. Maybe."

"That's what life's like. It changes on its own, if you let up on it."

But Esther didn't want a simple formula like this to speak to her, as other darker and more formidable things had. If the dark things had led to this dead end, the formula (life erases patterns as the sea does the sand ditch and castle) was not a valid pivot point, in spite of the fact that a pivot was necessary. Siri's wisdom would be bracketed, or bottled. Maybe it didn't need to be saved because Siri was a steady source. The sunniness of the Greeks, their practicality and self-sufficiency, were hers by nature. The excess of learning had not broken the sturdy motor that was a gift of Sybele's nature crossed with Dad's.

Esther took the second half of music history and theory. The library had outfitted a real listening room—a set of cubbies with turntables—so even when the room was empty, it felt more like a library and less like a cell. An undersized music major, clarinetist, befriended Esther.

Cecily insisted that Esther—even at this late date, and without playing an instrument—could minor in music. She spoke to Mr. Edelman. Couldn't Esther Ferry be a music writer or a historian?

Not if she can't play enough to study harmony, was Mr. Edelman's answer. So Cecily, whose pint-sized figure was the relic of a childhood battle with polio, persuaded Esther to take Piano for Winds and Strings—beginning piano. Sister Piano taught it and you could take it for two years, more than enough to play the Bach chorale-preludes in your sleep, and master the rudiments of theory and composition. Was it enough? Cecily asked Mr. Edelman, music advisor. He wasn't sure it would work, but Esther could take the courses, if she had room in her schedule. How far she'd get on no early training of the ear, or the hands, he couldn't say, but he was pessimistic.

Esther wrote twelve pages in her daybook that night, while Siri was reading a history play, her latest passion: Shakespeare, who went beyond the abstractions of philosophy to the realm of life on earth. Esther "screamed" onto her page notes on the delicious news from Mr. Edelman. Music had fallen onto her life like a heavy curtain, but it was all she was interested in. She wanted to live in its coils. There were no words in music, but there was thought— some—and an ecstasy of feeling. No one in life could produce so much—although the saints and crazy martyrs aimed at something of the same. Playing music, which Esther had never done with her own hands or lips, was its mimicry. The notes, which encoded the ecstasy, were read with the eyes and produced by the body to resound in the atmosphere for the sake of the ears and the little bones inside the skull. Playing music was a complete circuit of fulfillment. The stranger who created it in his head and encoded it on the page had deposited this precious energy for the ages. Now he was gone and the music, left in seed form, was the player's to grow in his own body.

"What are you doing?" Siri said, and then said it again. "Esther!"

"What?"

"What are you doing?"

Esther looked down at her hands. She didn't know, or couldn't explain. It took a minute to recollect. "I'm writing."

"I can see that, but what?"

"Nothing," Esther said, closing the book. "What are you doing?"

"Reading Shakespeare," she said, then added: "So don't tell me what you're writing. I don't care. Do you think I care?" Siri jumped off the bed and grabbed a towel and toothbrush.

Esther watched her go off in a huff. She reopened the daybook, but the thought had gone dead. How could she explain to Siri something she knew nothing about? That was part of the reason for the silence. The other part was she didn't want to.

Next day, Esther took her first lesson with Sister Piano, who offered two half-hour sessions per week to strings and winds, but Esther wanted a lesson every day. Sister Piano said no, two were more than enough. Esther could do the rest on her own. Sister gave her a key (she had a drawerful) to the practice room. Esther had a C-major scale and arpeggio to practice, and four sight-reading exercises. Sister wanted her to take the mimeographed sheets, but Esther begged to borrow the book, *Grade One,* and hurried over to the student union.

The practice room was a cube with nothing but a piano and bench. A window had been cut into the door and at first Esther just stood there, looking in.

Sitting on the bench, she stared at the keys. The room was soundproofed and a coolness emanated from the cement block walls. Esther opened her book and placed it, using the rock she found there, to keep the pages from closing. She curved her fingers and held them over the keys for the C-major scale; the left starting from the little finger and the right from the thumb. Her legs and arms were tingling. Her head was light. Touch it, she heard herself say, and the thumb dropped on middle C. Unbearably loud and rough-sounding, raggedy at the edges, as if the string knew some fool had dropped the hammer. Esther struck again, and tried this over and over, listening to the C, a heavy note, but full of brightness. She struck the key high up into its narrow root, and worked her finger by quarter inches down the smooth white tab to the overhanging lip, sounding the note. And out they came, a string of faintly uneven Cs. She struck hard and she stroked. She tried the thumb and the different fingers. She tapped twice, three times, and more multiples to hear how, as the muscles tired, the tone muddied. The little room was alive with overtones and echoes from the key strokes, a rosary of Cs—a cheap rosary of glass or metal beads, because the notes—even to Esther's untrained ear—were of inferior quality.

Someone was at the door. The half hour was up. Esther

folded her book, stuck the rock back on the music stand and exited. She stopped, though, just outside to listen. The student who had replaced her on the bench was causing a torrent of notes, doubled scales running up and down the keyboard. This sudden flowering of notes, after the drumming of Cs, was a miracle of multiplication and variety. Esther listened to the scales modulated from major to minor, and to the arpeggios that followed. She listened until the joy of it was unbearable. The rest of the world, to judge from the dull spaces around the practice room, was cold, colorless, noisy and crude. Esther checked the schedule on the wall outside the dining hall. She'd return at two thirty, when there was a free slot, and again from ten to midnight.

"I'm putting everything," she told Siri, who'd asked when she was planning to study for finals, "into my music."

What music? Siri might have asked, but Esther was too touchy these days to handle a tough or cynical question. How could Esther be playing "music" after one month of lessons with "Player" Piano, a halfwit, a sisterette, who hadn't been tapped to make her final vows, but functioned as a kind of servant to the teaching nuns, or "faculty," as they called themselves. The piano students took their lessons at the Longy School. And even then—as Siri knew, because she had a knack for doping out pecking order—the Longy deployed its lowest ranks to teach the musicians at St. M's. Just as in every other field, St. M's girls were treated like the dregs, less than mediocrities. And Esther didn't even seem to know this. To her, Sister Piano was a musical genius because she could sight-read the harmonies for Esther's stiff little melodies. Esther would polish up a two-phrase ditty by Handel or Bach, but almost always get it wrong. It sounded fine to Siri, who would hear Esther perform before her lesson—all the notes were there. She didn't miss any, or make mistakes, but Sister Piano always had a correction or criticism, and Esther would come back angry, frustrated, deflated. It was the fingering; it was the tempo; it was ignoring the rests, or skipping the codas; it was memorizing instead of sight-reading. Getting these kinks out of the music from *Grade One* took a month of practice. And Esther was practicing two to three hours a day— or whenever she could get the room. She was doing too much practicing, according to Player. She was practicing her mistakes. Sister wanted to restrict her practice to fifteen minutes a day, using a borrowed metronome and practicing one hand at a time.

"She's taking the joy out of it," Siri said, when she heard about the new regimen.

"No, she's not," said Esther, who defended Player, who wasn't even charging for the lessons.

Music was music was music, and Esther was playing it. Even Sister Piano fell in line after a while, and arranged for Esther to learn the Bartok "Mikrokosmos" for her recital piece; for practice, she had the notebook studies of Anna Magdalena Bach.

Esther was coming to music not as a backward pupil, but as a musician.

Between the practices, fifteen minutes at a time, and the hours in the listening room, or the language lab (where Esther did her ear training and started taking simple dictations), and the Friday afternoons at the Boston Symphony rehearsals, Esther was hardly ever around. Free time was spent cramming for the other four courses. She used the skim method she'd taught Siri, but there wasn't enough time, and she was writing essays on novels she hadn't finished, and taking quizzes on verb forms unknown. To be a music major, there was a juried audition, and against everyone's advice, Esther was going to try out. Sister Piano gave way to a young Korean from Longy. To pay for the lessons, Esther worked an extra day in the cafeteria. The Korean, only a few years older than Siri and Esther, practiced every spare minute— seven, eight, even nine hours a day. She crammed her students into one day a week and taught from seven thirty A.M. to nine P.M. Esther took a lesson at four.

Esther was afraid to tell Miss Paik what she had in mind as a pianist. To Miss Paik, wind and string players—the stupids who played a single line and thought that a marvelous feat of artistry—were the peons, the swine of the music world. An elephant foot had a more sensitive touch. Miss Paik's English vocabulary didn't include the word elephant, or foot, but Esther grasped her sign language, and was picking up the rudiments of Korean. She often supplied the tiny Asian musician, whose little hands could stretch the octave God knows how (perhaps they had been forced on the rack), with what she needed to express her contempt for American girls on fiddles and flutes. The piano was a sacred machine, and the calling to "play" it (Esther was sure that Korean had no equivalent for "play," but nine million variants for "work") was a gift of rare distribution. Every Korean child was called to the instrument, but even among those, few were chosen. No American child with a Catholic or Protestant parent received the tap. Americans were losing the ability to even hear the call, whose dialect, formerly with Polish and Russian accent, was shifting to the Orient.

How could Esther tolerate such rudeness, such snobbery? Siri wanted to know; but, according to Esther, the one with the hands was the one who called the shots. Miss Paik was to Esther a goddess of music.

Esther and Siri went to Boston to hear Miss Paik's senior recital at Longy. Esther was frozen with excitement, but it was also, Siri pointed out, a freezing cold day. Miss Paik had many pairs of furry gloves and an electric hand-warmer, but she'd told Esther, her worst student—but also her best in how much criticism she could take, and the sharp rate of improvement—that bathing them in hot water for twenty minutes was the only check against attacks from weather as cold and wet as Boston's in January. So she had a portable tank with a heating unit and hand towels from France. Her mother was coming from Seoul with a recital gown. A maid would take charge of the equipment. Normally, Esther told Siri, Miss Paik had to hire a student to haul the tank and the lotions and thermometer. But the maid had been caring for Miss Paik since she was a baby, and needed no instructions not to say the wrong thing or to let the water get cold before the soak time was up.

"How nervous she must be," Esther said at least half a dozen times on the shuttle, and on the subway, and on the walk to Longy.

"Why?" Siri asked, the first few times. "She knows it cold. You told me she could play this stuff in her sleep."

"You don't understand."

"What don't I understand?" said Siri, a student of Shakespeare.

"Even for Miss Paik, performance is an ordeal."

"So, why do it?"

"It's what she's been trained to do. She wants to do it."

"Well, then, don't call it an ordeal. If it's an ordeal, she's a masochist," Siri said. "Let me explain," she went on, before Esther could protest. "She hates people, she disdains them. No one understands music or its demands better than Paik, so why bother playing for an audience of imbeciles? If it's an ordeal."

"She's playing for her teacher," Esther said, remembering. "She's playing to get a concert manager."

"So, it's just a commercial exchange. She's selling her talent, just like everyone else who has something to sell."

"It's also for art. She'd like to make records to set her standard. Her Bach is all needles and pins. Wait'll you hear it. There's no air anywhere, no slack, no swatches of old-timey lyricism, no slop."

"How do *you* know?"

"That's what her friends say, her teachers, too."

"Paik has friends?"

"Well, you know what I mean. I've heard it, too. Maybe it's an ordeal, but it's well worth the pain. You'll see."

"I don't like Bach. You've played him for me, haven't you?"

"Don't compare!"

"Esther. Why have you made yourself into a baby just to do music? Didn't Paik say you'd never make it—even if you practiced fifteen hours a day for life?"

"That's not what she said."

They were at the door of the Longy School, a Victorian

manse with a deep porch. "Well, in her crazy words—same thing."

"I started too late," Esther said, as they entered, receiving the flood of notes from practice pianos on three floors.

"*I* started late!" Siri returned, blocking her ears. She hated noise, and only for Esther would she have come to Boston to be bored and assaulted.

"Yes, you started late and you'll always have—"

"Don't say it."

"You know you will."

"Will what?"

"You'll always have gaps."

"I can hide them!"

"They can't be hidden. Someone who started early will always know."

"Like you?"

"I'm not that far ahead. I started late, too."

"I don't mean music. I mean letters, knowledge, learning."

"We both started late."

"I started much later than you. I started last year."

Esther laughed. "You've come a long way."

"Can *you* see gaps?"

Esther thought a minute. Her body and mind were warmed by the scales and phrases and motifs and cadenzas pouring down the wide staircase. "I don't know. Maybe."

"What are they?"

Esther sat down on the bottom step. "Don't be discouraged," she said. (She didn't want to be a Miss Paik to poor Siri.)

"Tell me." Siri sat down.

"It's in the connections."

"What?"

"Everything you know is in boxes. What you know you know, Siri, but between the boxes—don't let this hurt your feelings—," Esther said, seeing the look on Siri's face, "there's nothing."

Siri swallowed. "So what?"

"That's what they'll notice."

"What if I keep my mouth shut and just talk out of these boxes, like we do for school?"

"It's in your writing, too, Sear."

"No, it isn't."

Esther thought about what Siri wrote for school. Her term papers and essay questions were pocked with details and dates and quotations and hard chunks of fact, but— although written in simple English—the prose was like broken pottery: sharp, uneven, obstructive, unsorted. It was a street that an aftershock had tumbled, and some diggers had come along and done the rough cleanup with dustpan and broom. And now Esther, thinking this, and Siri watching the thought with its depressing effect flitting across her face, had ruined the day for poor Siri. A judgment had been issued, as painful as the ones Miss Paik delivered at every lesson, but Esther was used to it, and Siri wasn't.

Teachers, parents—but especially friends like Esther— had spared Siri this view, as children are spared the sight of the mountain they're facing.

"What's supposed to be there?" Siri asked. It was a real question and she expected an answer.

"Where?"

"Between the boxes!"

People were drifting into the hallway, clustering there and displacing with their chatter the musical notes. The notes floated higher, Esther figured, because they were of lighter material. In that higher sphere, Esther could hear a phrase of a Bach that could only be Miss Paik warming up for the ordeal. It was needlepoint Bach, Esther had told her teacher, but Miss Paik, even when she understood what this craft was, was unimpressed by the comparison. But on this clear, frigid day, the tones were even finer. Perhaps silk embroidery was better and not the wooly stitches chewing up canvas. But— and *here* was something—for Miss Paik, as for Siri, the stitches were separate, no matter how closely placed, or how fast they rippled out: they let in cloth, dross, air, space. Miss Paik could not draw her notes into a smooth or unbroken line. Each note had an edge which constant practice and hypertrained ear had filed to a point, a blade, or—if it was an important note—a faceted diamond. There was something in Paik that refused to make the joins; to fuse the notes and make them yield a melody. They were too stiff-necked, like Paik. Too much practice had gone into each one. Too much discipline, attention, aggression even. They would not fold or slant or merge their unities, their egos, as they must.

People were gathering at the doorway of the recital hall, and still Siri was waiting for an answer.

"Never mind," Siri said. "I don't think you know either."

But Esther was sure she did know—no matter what it was. Clarity had this moment divided the musicians from the athletes, the faithful from the catechumens. Could this clarity be extended to cover whatever it was that Siri wanted to know?

"Boxes," Siri said, as they approached the doorway, "are not supposed to have something between them. That's what a box is. Boxes are not related to other boxes."

Esther knew she was angry, but the lights were dimming and the only seats left were in the front row, right underneath the flying wing of the grand piano.

During the concert—something crossed the stage in white and something else followed—the chilly hall was a solid block of stinging pressure, like sea air before a hurricane. With everything she had, Siri resisted it. Let it blow, let it rain. In the hard covert of her skull, she studied her boxes, opening them one by one and letting them air out. Each one was filled to brimming and, just as Esther said, filled with only one kind of thing. They were a pleasure to unpack: balls with balls, blocks with blocks, gyroscopes with gyroscopes, slinkies with slinkies, dolls with dolls, and the doll clothes separate. In her head there had been nothing and now there was this: the contents of a very small museum. She closed the boxes. It wasn't necessary to block the music for the sheer joy of viewing these boxes with their handy contents. Siri folded her arms, imagining herself stretched across them for a nap, and that's when she got it: what connected the boxes was herself!

Paik's pocked Bach had poked a thousand gold and silver pins into Esther's skin—hands and face, but also the parts wrapped in cloth, leather, or covered by hair. To keep

from crying from the pain of it, or the pleasure—
whichever it was—Esther conjured the concert as a whole-
body experience, so different from a 78 playing into an
empty practice room. Was it because they were sitting with
their heads in the guts of the concert grand? But Esther's
feet were on the floor and they, too, were hearing. Esther
felt the old self dropping like a skin of wax; underneath was
all vibrating nerve, new as a baby and just as wild, with no
discriminations, no categories. This was who was seated
under the grand piano.

Playing it was Annie Eiki Paik in a gown like a bandage,
wrapped from one shoulder to the opposite underarm; out
of this sleek cone were little toes hammering the pedals.
Paik upright, Paik bent at the waist until her nose was
brushing a black key, swaying and lifting an arm with hand
drooping, fingers dripping. She had caught Siri's eye with
those actressy moves, and Siri was set to laugh. It was during a quiet part, so quiet you could hear people breathing,
so the laugh was swallowed, but bubbled up again.

Siri couldn't look. It was too hilarious, especially from
her angle, where you could nearly see up the girl's nose.
And the faces she was making! Siri shut her eyes, but the
neat row of boxes was gone. This music was hellish. Siri felt
her teeth were being drilled. How much longer? It was
impossible to doze and there was something in the music
which made her think that lying across the boxes wasn't a
real connection, not the one philosophers would see as real.
She could lie or sprawl across them, but that didn't change
the contents of the boxes. Siri stiffened. Now she knew
what Esther had been trying to tell her—or maybe Plato

had, because now Siri could make better sense of that than of the gibberish that came out of Esther's head. The stuff in the boxes, so fine-sorted and neatly packed, contained only their own contents, and nothing at all of their thinker. She wasn't a thinker! She was a collector, a junkman. There was nothing personal or mindful about it. I'm just a stupid, stuck-up college girl, and barely that, she thought— although her grades were now good, and she was reading in and around her courses. Her grades were better than Esther's.

But what was a grade in this larger sense? (Was the concert over yet? No. Paik's arms were still flailing and feet pumping those slats under the piano. What did they do? Nothing.) The boxes had to be dumped out. They were nothing. They were an artifact. Start over. And Paik was starting over. Was she playing the same thing again? Siri looked at Esther, but Esther was asleep—an awful look on her face, as if she were grinding her teeth.

Siri wished she could sleep. Maybe sleep was the true origin of thinking. No one was in your sleep but you. The contents of the boxes were there, but reorganized—actually thrown all over the place with other things you hadn't collected, but arrived on their own. But real ideas were not formed by dreams. Nutty things were, and crazy stories that resembled parts of life, or the old days. Paik was playing a different kind of music now, and Siri could listen to it without flinching. It was airier, less like a fire alarm or an electric drill.

It was dreamy music. Siri looked at her program and counted down to number 2—Debussy—a name that sounded like powder or perfume: DuBarry, Patou, Tussy. This was easier to take, and Paik had become a different character on her chair, suspended above them. She'd stretched herself out and sat back on the bench, stroking the piano like a harp. She was a kook and why couldn't Esther see this? Siri looked at Esther. She was awake and, like Paik, elongated, all stretched out with her fingers extended on her lap. What was happening? Was everyone in the hall stretched out? Siri didn't think she could turn to look. She didn't want all those faces staring at her, or jolted out of their dreams, because that was what the music was doing. They weren't exactly asleep, but they were dreaming.

There were no ideas in this kind of dreaming. The stuff of it was as rich and juicy as night dreams, or as Siri's night dreams, which had always been a crazy zoo. These musical dreams had no words and the designs were just pretty patterns—or ugly crashes—but nothing you could do something with—faces and arms and trucks and steeples and fields of clover, or restaurants and amusement parks and dances. Music wasn't as bad as Siri had thought, but it wasn't good either. She had learned something about the state of her boxes—the whole of her learning, so far. But that was an accident. The music Paik was pounding out, or the snaky thing she was coaxing out, had not, of itself, toppled the empire of boxes. Time had done that. It was due to happen, because Siri was already bored with boxes, even though she hadn't quite pictured "boxes" as brain material until Esther named them. Knowledge couldn't be sorted, stacked and packaged, each thing by itself. Now she knew.

People were clapping and it was a relief to hear this natural sound. Siri turned to Esther with news on the tip of her tongue of the revolution taking place.

She turned to Esther, but Esther was gone. In Esther's place was a blob.

How can you be my partner in life, if I don't even know who the hell you are?—was Siri's thought, looking at Esther reduced to this. Siri wanted to slap her face, but the face, all gooey with glassy eyes and wax-white lips, you wouldn't want to touch. Your hand might stick to its gummy surface. Esther wasn't even seeing out of her eyes. They were open, but nothing was in them but a sheen.

Out of her seat she leapt, scaring Siri out of her wits. If something this lifeless could spring like that—no wonder people, even young people, had heart attacks. Siri's heart was racing; even the air was jazzed from the bounce. Out of her seat and flying along the aisle in front of the audience, scooting into a door next to the stage.

Siri sat down. She collected the two purses, but left the programs. If Esther didn't care, why should she? She turned to watch people flooding out of the hall. Some scurried up to follow Esther through that side door. Where did it lead? Maybe there was a Coke machine back there, or a restroom. Siri wasn't thirsty and didn't have to go. She sat and watched two guys unlock the wheels and roll the piano to the back of the stage, then cover it with a green blanket, strapped to its legs. Someone pulled a curtain down, hiding the big piano from sight. Haul that elephant away, and put it to sleep.

The hall was quiet, but something was going on elsewhere.

Esther knew her life was over. By rights, it shouldn't even be half over, but it was finished. She had long ago forgotten where she came from. Waltham—yes, she remembered that. Esther Ferry, 42 Pine St., Waltham, Mass., and the telephone number. It was there if she needed it, but it was like the dog tags of a dead soldier. She was ferried over the Styx by Paik, that dark soul, and awake in this new world dominated not by words but by numbers—intervals, circle of fifths, half tones, triads, the mathematical conundrum of equal temperament. Number was the essence, but also just the skin or waxed paper of music. Someone had to call it something, to measure it with something, but once inside its skin, numbers dropped away. Here on this new shore, there were no numbers. Music shone free in its round basin. Esther gazed upon it—not with her eyes but with memory, which was feeling.

At first, Eiki Paik failed to recognize her pupil from St. M's. When she didn't offer her tiny paw to shake, Esther grabbed it and wrapped its powdery baby flesh in both of hers.

"Oh, it's you," Paik said.

Esther sang a song of pure praise to the artist. At first Paik didn't know what she was talking about—talking so fast, and Paik was tired and ready to be gathered up by her mother, with her coat, music and portable tank. There was a reception in the Longy salon and Mrs. Paik, thinking Esther a friend, invited her. And here was the teacher, an ancient lady in a velvet cape, who stood with her face close to Paik's and issued of stream of nothing but criticism. Paik stood and took it. The crone chewed through the concert.

And here was Siri, whose existence Esther had forgotten, planting herself in earshot of this hot stream, so ugly and hurtful. What Siri heard was a dreamlike confirmation of her own views. "The Bach," as the teacher put it, was played like a sewing machine. Paik was crying now and so was Esther, but Siri aligned herself with this sharp old lady, turning to tell her—but she had already flown off—how right she was.

"But what about the Debussy?" Paik bawled.

"It was fine," the old bat said, over her shoulder.

So, this was music—a life sentence to endless hours of pure boredom, and then this theater of punishment. Thinking about it, Siri liked it better. It was a battleground comically uneven. One side was the player, practicing a lifetime for a one-shot match; the other side was this circus crowd with their ideals, forever disappointed by the pathetic specimen rolled out: the individual case, ordeal, senior recital. It was the ugliest and the unfairest game Siri had ever seen, but it was funny, it was the comedy of comedies.

Paik was shuffled off by two Korean ladies. She looked back over her shoulder and saw something. Siri? Esther? Siri thought it was Siri, Esther Esther, but behind them was the music teacher, digging in her purse for something, ready to strike again. And there was Esther, approaching her, tapping her on the shoulder, to get whatever she hadn't already dished out to Paik. Siri couldn't believe her ears. Esther was asking this cutthroat, this Attila, for music lessons.

7.

And so life became for Esther two things like two halves of a wheel: making the money for the lessons with Miss Barringer, and taking them. For sleep, Esther practiced. Siri observed this experiment because it exceeded understanding. She couldn't ask Esther about it because Esther didn't understand it either. A funny smile would curl, eyes would cloud over and dumb things fall out of her mouth. Sampler wisdom, proverbs, golden rules, five of this and three of that. The spells and mantras from legendary piano pedagogues, and the weekly lessons to pound it all in. Every week—every day—Esther was losing vocabulary; her sentences were shrinking and all were declarative or imperative. The old clausal, accumulative and dialectical Esther, with a native tongue that coiled and knotted like a barrelful of snakes, was now stupefyingly simple. The key to a seamless trill was "four over five." Five with one hand, four with the other. Five what? Four what? Siri didn't know, but she listened because the key to this life had to be somewhere and maybe one of these gnomic incantations would give the hint. Or maybe four or five of them strung together. Two things had happened that were incontrovertible: Esther was a robot and Esther was happy. Esther didn't want to interrogate this life as a philosophical case because it wasn't.

There was no intellectual matter here, no free will, no power of mind to give the law, and Esther had admitted as much before she went under. Less philosophical, it was more a case of psychopathology, of sensory deprivation, brainwashing, or all three.

Esther woke up at four thirty to open the cafeteria for the cooks and servers, who came in at five. Food service had promoted her to manager because she was reliable, had a short commute and never came to work drunk or high. She had no police record, so bonding was not a problem. Early on—before Esther went robotic—she had said that the food services kingpin had urged her to consider a career in commercial or even industrial food because she had, as he put it, "smarts and stamina," and wasn't "a goddamn fool, pervert or crook."

Esther liked the work, or didn't dislike it, because the practice rooms were locked until eight and it paid well. At eight, she tore off her uniform for the wraparound skirt and black sweater she wore day in and out, and collected her music, waiting for the janitor to unlock the three piano rooms. Esther called the pianos Inky, Betty and Lady Pamela. Inky was an upright with real ivory keys, silky to the touch but, overall, a tuneless wonder, Betty was a spinet with a hard action and metallic tone, and Lady Pamela was a baby grand, a Steinway. This was the piano rolled out for recitals. The college had no concert grand, but even Eiki, who still taught Esther on off days—she was backup to Miss Barringer—liked to play it. The action was ideal and when tuned, it stayed tuned. It had personality—

not all pianos do, Eiki told Esther so many times. It had depth, subtlety and didn't betray, as so many instruments did, in the clinch.

Esther had Lady Pamela for thirty minutes, but she was not ready for her. Hands were swollen and stiff, muscles knotty from yesterday's practice and the morning's hauling, chopping, stirring and shaping. Sometimes she lay her hot cheek on Lady's cool white fingers, sleeping there, or listening to the piano strings chiming on their own—overtones and harmonics, the music of the spheres. Before the half hour had elapsed, though, Esther had flexed her fingers and rippled through two or three series of major and minor scales. The first sounds of the day had a clean, cool taste. Esther listened to each tone for all the tones within, sympathetic notes sounding elsewhere in Pam's large, wooden chest. Pam was music in and of herself and until the moment when Esther started practicing an actual piece and causing the piano to stutter and choke, to swallow notes, or have one run over another, Esther's morning music was perfect. Five to ten minutes of the half hour were mostly the piano's, the best music of the day. Then Esther set to work. Before long, she was saddled on Betty for the first hour of piece-work. Betty was nasty in her accuracy. She spat back whatever Esther pumped in. The harder Esther tried to make her notes sing, to play four or five legato, strung together, or leaning into each other like barbs in a feather, the harder Betty worked to pop them out like gumballs and BBs. If you could make Betty sing, you could play the ribs of a garbage can. Everyone knew this, but with

Esther, Betty played her worst. An hour with Betty and Esther was in tears, but had to haul off to her first class in ear training.

There were five students in ear training, none particularly gifted—no perfect pitch, or even perfect relative pitch—but none as backward as Esther. Mr. Moriarty, ninety years old and an uncle of the president, who earned half his keep by rehearsal piano and light groundskeeping, played melodic dictations and heard rhythmic recitations. Esther listened hard, she replayed the intervals in her head against the mnemonics other students had taught her: Beethoven's fifth, the notes of a door chime, "Arrivederci Roma," "Taps." She nailed one—maybe the first, maybe the last—wrote the note on her staff paper. What were the others? They were lost.

Over time, she could retain the tune, but got lost pinning down the intervals between notes 2 and 3, or 3 and 4, trying so hard to keep the tune from fraying at either end. When she tried to explain this to Siri, Siri jumped on the bed, singing "Hold That Tiger." But it wasn't funny. It was a disaster. Esther was flunking ear training, even with all the extra work she was putting in, playing intervals in her head and on the keyboard. No dictation by Esther received a passing grade. And the class had passed on to harmonic dictation; one student was ready for counterpoint. Esther was drowning, and "Get out while you can," which Siri offered as advice, was no help at all.

Afternoons were devoted to music history, theory, and choral training. Esther was an alto, but her voice was not strong or true. After chorus, she went back to the cafeteria for the supper serve and cleanup. When the kitchen and dining room were finally cleared and scrubbed, reeking of Ajax and steel wool, ammonia and bleach, Esther was bushed. The cook had a couple of kerosene lamps and these were set on a table in the windowless prep room. The cards came out and Esther played a few hands of hearts or gin rummy. The cook, a heavy man with a wife and a houseboat and an ancient Nash Rambler, had a thing for Esther, and everyone in the kitchen knew it. They kidded her and warned her about the late nights in the prep room, but it was just cards, Esther told them, and it was relaxing after the long day of strain and failure. They played real games until the dishwashers and salad lady went home and then it was just one or two hands of Old Maid and Slapjack to finish off the night and the six-pack Hank kept behind the milk jugs. "It's not hurting anyone," Esther said, when a nutrition student spotted it.

From the cafeteria, Esther went home and collapsed. Siri wanted to talk and Esther, dozing and waking up while Siri made her points, let her. Siri was reading *The Tragedy of King Richard the Third* and thinking about writing her own tragedy. *Richard III* was a lifelike play; at least it reminded Siri of her life. If you want to get anything done, and done right, you had to get other people out of the way. It takes talent and it takes guts.

Esther was awake enough to hear the name of the play and, knowing it from her days in English, said she thought it was a shallow play, almost stupid in its single-minded action. Richard was not complex like the Henrys or even the royal Macbeth.

"That's what I like about it," Siri said. "The play is one line, one arrow, yet it holds the reader's interest."

"He gets it in the end, though, doesn't he?"

"'My kingdom for a horse.'"

Siri was doing nothing but reading. In classes, she kept a book on her lap, listening with one ear for the "pearls" that were rare as hen's teeth in the St. M's lecture halls. Dr. Farrand liked the sound of his own voice. Siri watched his feet stride across the stage. He walked and talked, reminding Siri of a Chatty Cathy doll with eyelashes and spongy hair and eyes that clicked open and closed. Dr. Farrand loved to talk in a stylish way. Siri's reading, once she'd started alternating Shakespeare with philosophy, made room for style. Plato was not too stylish, not to her ear. Socrates was a pedant with a scolding tone. His analogies and metaphors, no matter how fancy, were always made for battering home a point to some gullible Greek with nothing better to do than follow Socrates around on his walks. "Gasbag," Siri had pencilled in the margins of "Republic VI," but Book X was like something out of *2001*: Plato was finally airborne. This was style, but style was also Shakespeare every time he opened his mouth. Shakespeare was all words and bouncing lines, sharp retorts and deep jokes. The stories were good, but Siri loved the style. And now that she knew style as well as anyone living, she could see how stylish a speaker Dr. Farrand was, especially when he was striding up and down the stage.

Siri started collecting his words. She had a notebook for "pearls." On her lap was the book she was reading in tandem. Farrand was talking about Richard and Siri was reading Descartes' *Meditations.* René was a Richard-type—this much she could see. What he did to the ancient philosophers, Richard did to the king and the king's children and his own brothers and sisters. The difference was that when René eliminated his forebears, he had enough energy left to collect his thoughts. When Richard was finished, he was a nervous wreck and Shakespeare steamrolled him with armies and navies that came out of nowhere. Richard had nowhere to go: he was a destructive fool, but René had a reason to clear the field. He cleared the field for himself to think in peace. He started with square one. Because Siri had started with square one, Thales, she loved this kind of beginning. She never got tired of beginning with a new beginning: water, flux, cogito, ideals—they were the basics. They were better than stories, even Shakespeare's stories, but style in Shakespeare was better than philosophic style, so Siri felt it was not asking too much to read all the plays and to listen to Farrand's spiels.

Farrand liked to take something Richard said and turn it inside out. He liked complication, which was the opposite of Siri. While he worked his fifty lines of thought, Siri pulled her cable. Which was better? Farrand had better words and more tortured sentences, but Siri's idea was clearer. She could fit the whole of this play into a thimble. Dr. Farrand laced himself up in his lines. Was it a cocoon, a spider's web or just a big snarl? Siri would like to ask him— to put it to him, because he was a ham and begging for a put-down—but Esther had never taught Siri how to talk. She could write and think, but public speaking was its own art, and Siri was smart enough to know that, at this, she was still a dumbhead, so she kept silent and Dr. Farrand talked on.

Was he cute? Siri squinted. In a way he was, when he took the trouble to dress up in a suit and picked out a decent tie. His shoes, which caught Siri's eye and held it, were dreamy. Why? What was it about a man's shoe? Siri went to Dad's closet in her mind and sorted out his shoes: beat-up tennis shoes, "brogans"—thick soles, brown leather— black wingtips, old black wingtips, loafers, boat shoes, golf shoes, tan bucks and dancing pumps, which Dad never wore, but Sybele kept polished for benefits and holiday balls. Dad's shoes were big and smart and he had nice socks—you never saw an inch of hairy flesh—but they weren't stylish like Dr. Farrand's. Siri wished she had better eyesight or binoculars, but from here they looked like one seamless piece of leather, and the soles were thin. Siri watched the shoes slap across the boards. Were they English? Dad had bought a pair of English shoes in college and he was still talking about them. Where were they? Some dog he owned ate one, Sybele said. It was his best pair of shoes, the kind of thing, he liked to say, that you indulge yourself in once and only once.

Dr. Farrand had indulged himself more often because Siri noticed at least two different-colored leather shoes and one suede. The suedes were probably bucks, but even these were on their own high level: smooth, pliable and hugging the arch in an exciting way—at least to look at.

The two styles went together: the shoes and Shakespeare, the words and the steps. He was cute, and better than that, he was cool. No wonder Esther liked him, but

Esther didn't know the half of it. How could she when her father bought his shoes at Thom McCann.

Was Siri falling in love? She watched a gaggle of idiots surround Dr. Farrand after class. He pushed up his glasses and rubbed his eyes. He smiled at the gaggle. They were like chickens or fleas. He sat on the edge of the platform, and Siri could hear his voice from where she sat. She waited until he finished, and two by two, the gaggle dispersed. Siri looked the other way. Why acknowledge these fools, or pretend they were in the same league as herself? Sure enough, waiting in place, not moving a muscle, the mountain came to Mohammed, as the saying goes, and Siri was starting to know some sayings. He stood at the end of her row. "Were you waiting to speak to me?" was the best he could do. Lame.

Siri reeled him in. Was it the silence, the sulk or the stack of books?

"Did you like my lecture?" he asked, sitting down one seat away.

"I like the play," she said.

"It's a great play. It's the best of the second-tier tragedies," he said, taking the teacherly tone he'd used on the fleas.

"It's a great play period," Siri said, gathering the books. There was another stack under the chair.

"I think we've met before, haven't we?"

Siri looked at Dr. Farrand. She'd have to bring him up to speed. Otherwise, it was a waste of time. "You took my roommate out on a date a year ago."

"Who's your roommate?" he asked, smiling his hardest.

"She's a music major now. She dropped English."

"I know who you mean now. Was her name Sheryl or something?"

"Yeah."

"That wasn't a date. Faculty aren't supposed to date students, last I heard."

"But you're not real faculty, are you?"

Dr. Farrand reddened up to the hairline, so Siri knew she had hit the spot.

"What do you mean?"

"You're not on the real faculty here. You're a grad student from somewhere else."

"That's not really your business, is it? I don't think you're even registered for my class."

"I'm not."

"Well, do you have someone's permission to take it, and sit here harassing me?"

"You're not Catholic either. I don't even know how you got in."

"Just who do you think you are!"

"My family," Siri said, feeling her way through this with a goal now in sight, "happened to give a lot of money to this school, and they have a real interest in the faculty. They named the library after my granddad."

Dr. Farrand was silent. Siri knew he was stretched over the first barrel and ready for the next.

"You're quite a reader," he said, as she stood up, grappling with the stacks of books.

"This is nothing. You should see what I have at home."

Dr. Farrand was still sitting. He looked tired.

"Goodbye for now," Siri said, stepping over his legs.

He stood. "What do you mean, 'for now'?"

"Why would you want to do it?" Esther asked. She was working with her pitch pipe, because after fifteen minutes, Siri refused to blow the set of notes that Esther could never get right, no matter how hard she tried.

"I don't know. Stop that a minute, will you? You're hurting my head. I can't think."

But Esther couldn't stop, so she took the pitch pipe outside, but Siri could still hear it. "Go to the bathroom and play!" she yelled through the door.

A minute later, Esther was back. You couldn't play the pitch pipe without seeing or feeling the notes. It didn't work as a test.

"What would you say if I told you I was going to fall in love and get married—or at least get him to ask me?" Siri said. She was looking at herself in the mirror, but all Esther could see was the side of her head—hair and the tip of the turned-up nose. Siri was very pretty these days, although thin as a straw. In the trips to Boston, she had recalculated her wardrobe, selecting black pencil skirts and white sweaters. Her hair was long and thick, dirty blond, and she often pulled it into a schoolmarm knot, flattering to the baby face and white-blue eyes. The annual winter flu had given her a translucent pallor. Compared to Esther, whose unbound hair was an Afro and who'd bulked up again from all the sitting at the piano, she was——. There was no comparison. Esther got up to stand at the mirror.

"Aren't you going to ask me why?" Siri said, deeply absorbed in the mirrored image.

"Why?"

"Because I want to," Siri said, "because I can. And also because——" She caught sight of Esther's head in the mirror. From the look on her face, Siri knew she believed it. "I need to know what it's like."

"What what's like?"

"To fall in love. To feel that way."

"Oh, you're going to feel it, too? I thought it was just him."

"Plato says it's the penultimate thrill."

"That's not what Plato says."

"Yes he does. I know him much better than you do."

"Love to Plato doesn't mean what you think it does, Siri. He'd never use the word 'thrill.' I love music," she went on. "That's Plato's idea of love."

"Wrong. That's infatuation," Siri said. She had pulled the ribbon tying the bun and spread the soft hair around her shoulders like a shawl. It was exactly the hair she needed for what she had to do. No bleach or perms or brush rollers had broken a thread. When it was clean—not too often to preserve its protective oils—it was a glowing halo. It was velvety to the touch and shone like polished wood. The hair alone was a magnet.

Esther was whistling into the pitch pipe. She stopped. "You're doing it just to compete with me," she said, first taking the pitch pipe out of her mouth.

Siri was regarding her throat. It was white. The collarbone was like the spread wings of a dove. She had a silver necklace with a tiny bell. The bell dropped like a bird's head into that perfect throat hollow. "I'm completely purged now," she said, "of the 'false friends' of mental life. Whatever happens to me now," she said, "will make a lasting impression."

"Did you hear what I just said?"

"No. I didn't."

Siri hadn't articulated her reasons until she saw the pattern in the mirror because she was a pattern—the symmetry was perfect at this moment. She was thin but not gaunt, young but not stupid, pretty but not dazzling, sentient but not sensitive, proud but not vain, self-satisfied but not smug. Books were now her life, but reading Shakespeare had shown the need for experience—like the grit that makes the pearl. Or was it the scouring action of adversity? She had to launch this self into the unknown, but not the way Esther had done it, with her face to the wall, shying at shadows. Siri would face the direct sun, or whatever star it was, and be blinded.

Turning away from the mirror, she saw the child with the pitch pipe. This is what she had outgrown. "It's not what you know that's important, it's what you do with it."

"Are you talking to me?" tiny Esther said.

"I just hope this isn't too easy for me," Siri said. "That would take the fun out of it."

"Are you in it for the fun, or the learning?"

Siri looked back into the mirror at both faces. "It's not like a book, Esther. In life, the fun *is* the learning."

"The fun is never the learning, Siri. You got that wrong."

"Shakespeare said it, not me."

"I think you're wrong about that, too."

"In that case, wrong thinking is the only way to have experience!"

Esther sat on the bed, her face falling out of the mirror. "I never thought of it that way, but you could be right."

In his classes and on his stage, Dr. Farrand was doing the best acting of his career. More and more students were sitting in on his classes, even if they had to cut their own. A couple of the nuns with a free period sat in the back. Word had got out, and even they had heard it.

Shakespeare the clinician, Shakespeare the hangman, Shakespeare the woman and Shakespeare the man; the priest, the joker and the jack of all trades. Did Farrand think he was Shakespeare? Or just one of the characters with a big role and time alone on the stage? He could speak all the parts and some from memory. He shouted and scolded and strutted and struck a pose. There was no need to run the projector for a glance at Olivier and Gielgud, Welles and Richardson. Dr. Farrand could do them, too. Siri begged Esther to bag just one of the choir rehearsals and watch, and she did.

"You had to see it," Siri said as they walked out.

"Yeah. I guess I did."

"It's all for me."

"You think so?" If Esther hurried, she'd get Betty before the other musicians got out of choir.

"Do you doubt it?"

"I'm afraid to."

"But you might, if you weren't afraid?"

"I'm afraid of you."

"Do you doubt it?"

"I've got to run."

Siri turned back to the auditorium. She waited for Dr. Farrand in the projection room. The assistant had packaged up the films, but knew to let Siri in before locking the door. Through the window, Siri could see "Call-me-Tim," as she called him, knifing through today's gaggle. This was hard for him, Siri knew, but it was little enough to ask for the gift of her own time. And it was a gift—that's what he told her in his own words. Siri had jotted down the phrase.

And here he was, Callmetim.

"Hi," he said, dropping into a chair. "Come sit on my lap."

"I don't feel like it."

"Please."

"Ask me later."

"Can we go somewhere together?"

"Where?"

"Anywhere."

Siri and Farrand had never ventured off campus—or on, for that matter, because Siri didn't want the nuns or the students nosing around. They stayed in the projection room for the hour before Farrand had to go to his next class.

Siri wanted to fall in love, but so far, she couldn't make herself, and he was having no luck either, no matter what he said or did. They could both tell it wasn't working, but the time spent together in the stuffy room was digging Farrand in—or so he said—deeper and deeper.

When he wasn't reciting, Siri could barely stand him. Reciting the sonnets especially was Farrand at his best.

Everything else was inferior. Why? Siri hadn't told him how far off he was from her expectations, but he was getting the idea. "You never want to kiss me," he said, and his face looked sad. But he was an actor, and that's what Siri told him. "Don't act."

"I'm not acting. I'm hurting. I long for you."

Siri looked through the projection window. The next class was filing into their seats. This was medieval dramatic romance. Farrand begged her to stay for that class. After, they could talk more, but Siri didn't care for any of these fake-folkloric plays. There were the classics, the philosophers and Shakespeare. Farrand's other fields were religious palaver. The Dark Ages were called dark for a reason; and it stayed dark until Dante, and to tell the truth, there wasn't much light there either. It stayed dark. Siri and Esther—when they had time to talk—liked to say this. It got dark after the Romans, was the prompt.

And it stayed dark! was the reply. Esther was catching on. She wasn't as thick as Siri had thought, although the music had rotted her brain.

Farrand locked his arms around Siri's stringlike frame. "I want to make love to you," he said in a hoarse tone. He was acting again.

"I'm too young for that," she said, wriggling away, but also testing the strength of his hold: he wasn't even trying.

"Fool," she added.

"Why do you torment me?" he said. "And now I'm late."

Siri looked out the window. The hall was only half filled because this class was pure lecture: no movies, no acting, and it wasn't even in real English. She had no use for these dinosaur languages: pre-English and pre-French. They were hard, funny-looking and dull to the ear. Garbage talk, she called the middle languages, and Farrand took the insult. "It's not me, not the real me," he said, but Siri knew he was acting.

She was looking out this porthole, watching the hall slowly fill. "Go ahead," she said. "Go down and teach your class."

"What are you going to do?"

"I'm going to watch you."

He was silent. "Please don't."

"I'm going to watch you from up here. If you look up, you'll see me and I'll make you laugh."

Farrand was late, but he stood there, gazing at Siri. "Kiss me."

"Go."

"I'll be back."

Siri shut the door behind him and clicked the lock. She was in the projection room and it felt right. She was well above the gaggle and had Farrand—now on stage—in her line of sight. The lights were shining in his eyes when she turned the projector on and aimed the beam. A movie was playing on his face. *Henry the Fourth,* or that's what it looked like, Orson Welles as fat Falstaff. No matter how hard she tried to experience life as it played on her skin, as other people said they felt it, life proved as vaporous as this beam. She could think about everything, but experience was just this play of light.

Maybe she hadn't been at it long enough. She turned off the projector, playing with a strand of film while looking at

Farrand through the focusing lens, watching him talk with no sound. Up close, his face was expressionless, even when it was in motion. She could see from a distance that he didn't really believe what he was saying. He was a fake. The words didn't mean anything to him. There was no registration. He was like a fog horn.

This discovery had to be as profound as any made by philosophers, but it wasn't philosophy. Was it psychology? Dr. Farrand, unlike Esther, was not in his body, or at least, not in his head. He was lecturing to this class, but his life was going on (if he had a life) elsewhere.

Siri was eager to see if his life might be going on with her, so she waited and after an hour, he came bounding up the stairs and they "made love," as he called it, on the floor of the projection room. It was a hellish experience, like something on an operating table or in a morgue.

"I love you," he said, when he was finished, and Siri was hurting and hurting bad. She barely heard him. "What'd you say?"

"I love you."

Dr. Farrand had to go. There was a make-up class at another college somewhere in Boston. He was expected there, but he'd be back.

Siri was sore, bleeding onto the wooden floor four purple drops. Dr. Farrand offered to find paper towels and bring them back, but that's all the time he had. Was she all right?

Siri didn't know how to answer this question and, in the interval, Dr. Farrand had his pants on. He left his handkerchief just in case she needed it. She took it and draped it over her face.

"Aren't you getting up?" he said at the doorway. "Get up! Get up off the floor."

Siri stayed down. She wasn't moving until she had a formulation for what had happened, or even a name to call it. It was an equation, or at least, there was an equals sign in there somewhere, or a set of cancelling arrows, one going one way, one another. That's all she had formulated. The door was closing. It was a metal door and Siri heard it screech and chunk. As it entered its frame, there was a final, satisfying click, as the rhomb of a lock slicked into a hole.

Waiting for the formulation, Siri sorted through the junk of purely teenage response. She was still capable of it. She'd been laid or "porked." The pickle had been dipped, the rocket polished. She hadn't seen rocket or pickle. She'd felt it, though, and it wasn't pleasant. It felt like a full balloon whose skin rubbed and squeaked against her own skin—if it was skin that she had down there. She knew it was dark red, gizzardy red. That was the color of the fold into which the balloon had been crammed, till she thought her head would burst from pressure. The rocket itself was mushy at first, but then like a model car or model plane without the wings.

The floor was cold and Siri's legs and behind were bare against it. Her skirt was bunched up in a sweaty, salty ball. She smelled like a monkey cage. All this was clear, but nothing was formulated. The experience corresponded to nothing in life, except maybe the time Siri had been hit on her bike by a slow-moving car, or when she'd fallen from a tree onto the split-fail fence, or into the frigid water between Uncle Duke's and Mr. Kaplan's boats.

It wasn't fun, but Siri was too smart to think it was going to be. The idea of it didn't sound fun, and when people mentioned it, they were embarrassed, or tried to embarrass each other. What was it good for besides having babies? If it was the whole point of growing up, having dates, being a lady or not being a lady, it wasn't much. Believing in Santa Claus was better; even the Easter Bunny had something going for it—not so much the tooth fairy or godmothers.

Siri knew Dad liked it. He had a stash of magazines and dirty books. (Teddy had found them behind other books in the den-library. Teddy said he liked this kind of thing, but Siri knew he was showing off.) They *were* exciting, but Siri didn't know why, since all they had were pictures of nude women with smarmy expressions, and hair a mess, dyed too blond or teased and left uncombed. Why were they exciting? Anything Dad liked was usually good, but this was something he hid. Sybele's magazines were about knitting and gardening and raising polite children. She got Book of the Month Club in the mail, but there was no sex in any of those books.

Siri thought about the word. She was shivering, but the formulation was barely begun. She managed to pull her narrow skirt over her injuries. (She didn't want to look: too gross.) Sex wasn't much of a word, and when Shakespeare used it, calling it "the sex," he was referring to the female of the species—that's what Esther had said when Siri asked.

Sex and the Single Girl was a famous book title, but no one she knew had read the book. It was risqué, people said, but it was also low-class, like reading the *National Enquirer,* or *Argosy,* for men.

The word wasn't philosophical; it was scientific, and it sounded like it belonged in the hospital, or maybe in religion, like Extreme Unction, a sacrament and the last one you got. To Descartes, or even to Kant, it meant nothing. Plato didn't name it, but he knew what it was. Plato was very human in his way, as if he knew more than he could say, or felt like saying. The Pre-Socratics were as primitive as those funny, one-celled things that could be either fish or vegetables. For them, sex was like antifreeze, something they hadn't heard of, but had to use just to keep the species going. In the future, it would become real, something they could name and think about.

Siri thought she might be able to move, gather herself off the gritty floor, where she'd been bleeding to death, and see about the rest of life. The projection room was creepy, airless and claustrophobic, but she liked it. It felt homey, especially now that it offered shelter in dire need. I'm hurt, therefore I am. This was the simplest equation. (Were two propositions enough to make it a syllogism?) Syllogism or not, it was the right one.

Did the pain—and the anger that spread over it like a tide—create something original like the proposition Descartes came up with? Or was it just run-of-the-mill vicissitude? That it had been seeded in the projection room might entitle her to a larger claim. In a bed, where it happened to most people, it was as ordinary as eating a hotdog in a roll. This was more like a clam roll, the first time a clam roll was created out of nothing. Who would think, for instance, that inside a shell case was some ooze that could be fried, once you found it, and after you dipped it in bread crumbs, and stuffed it into a hotdog roll? Ergo, which meant therefore. If you applied ergo to the originary clam roll, what followed could be a claim to an original thought. And people would understand it, too—not that Siri cared in the least about "people." Never mind. As a snack, once it was created, people liked it. Even landlocked people who lived in the "bread basket" (which is what the nuns called the Midwest) had heard of clam rolls.

For the formulation, Siri had three quantities: pain, the clam roll and the agency of a faculty member with a stylish way of talking. She herself was the "ground," the a priori, the entity upon which you could count, but also the material of the action, the thing it happened to.

Siri knew that her first dialogue would, like Plato's, be on love. Not that this was love. This was more like an accident. It might have happened just as it did, or not. It could have been delayed or even avoided. That it had happened created the instance for formulation, and the awakening that flowered out of that mental motion. Now, she said, gazing at the wrinkled wool of her skirt (of course, it had to be a pale violet; so, ergo, wrecked), I am alive.

Sex was the answer to the question of existence. That cut both ways, she thought. It's true in the obvious sense for the species, but, for me, it's the crux. Everything falls from it.

I am myself, she thought, the injured party, but I am also

this circulating wisdom, which viewed the whole thing and absorbed its meaning.

The formulation was perfect: it was elegant and simple (although clam rolls could be messy), and Siri was free to leave the scene. It hurt to walk, but it was dark now, it was late, and she could hide what she didn't want other people to see. The "problem of other minds," something philosophers worried about, was simply this: that they couldn't keep their noses out of other people's business. Luckily, though, thought was hidden, so they'd never see that under a bloody skirt—which they could see—a miracle had occurred.

So why was Siri crying? Was it because she was already pregnant and moody? Was it because, "porked," she was ruined for life? She cried all the way to the new dorm, and the modern cement cell-block she shared with Esther. She passed "people" in the form of the housemother, gabbing on the switchboard phone, and someone ironing in the smoker, and went into the empty room. No Esther, but she was never there.

Siri now had her own phone. She looked at it. Sybele had forced it on her. When the roommates were reading, or Esther was sleeping, they pulled the plug out of the jack. It didn't matter: they never answered it, because it was always Sybele on the other end. The Ferrys still made no long-distance calls.

Siri dialed home—the main number—but when Teddy said hello, she hung up. I am not talking, she said out loud, to that runt. Teddy was smart, but this was way over his head: he had no philosophical education to speak of. He was a scientist at heart and, although the scientific method had derived from Descartes, he didn't know that. Like most modern people, he took it all for granted. What? That the underpinnings of any kind of method were fragile, hand-made, essentially subjective. All of that, in his male arro-gance, he didn't know. Was Siri going to pop his balloon right then and there——? The thought of that word, "bal-loon," made her sick. There were now words and ideas and silhouettes and body parts that could never be brought to mind: they were outlawed. Anything beginning with *F* or *P* or *S,* but also certain sensations and a whole roll of memory like a cartoon, Felix the cat and Tweety, or Elmer Fudd and Bugs, Nancy and Aunt Fritzi. All this had to go into an unla-beled box marked with a skull and crossbones or a red *X* in a circle. Gone——and it was gone.

How could it be gone if there was still this gored wool skirt hanging from her waist ("gored" was troubling even though it began with *G,* so into the box it went), that was clotted with dried sweat and purple blots? The skirt's lining (Siri had the hem in her hand) was pure silk and in front, it was still okay, perfect, although wrinkled; it was sewn into the skirt so the bright side was out and the smooth side next to the skin. This was thoughtful of the dressmaker; a touch that Siri could appreciate now that the silk fell so lightly over the hurt legs. This was courtesy, graciousness, a touch of elegance that no one could see. But if Siri spread her still-vibrating legs, she could see that the back of the lining was spotted and grubby, as if a muddy fist had grabbed it. There was a small hole where a thread had broken and, now slack, went waffling backwards toward the hem. A lifetime of work went into making a skirt so perfect—Villager or Cos Cob—shaving the sheep (first growing it, feeding it and fencing it in), carding and spinning, weaving, cutting, making the pattern out of thin paper, printing instructions on it and stuffing it in an envelope with a picture of the skirt on the cover, making ten thousand of them in a factory, importing the silk from China, putting the inside and outside together, shipping to Bonwit's or Best, putting a tag on it and hiring the salesgirl to sell it to a mother of a college girl. These skirts were the pure thing-in-itself, Siri thought, crying a little, but starting to dry out, which felt worse. The tears were like unbroken thought, but the dry misery replacing them was harsh and crumbly ground. Nothing grew on it. Thought stopped short, broken like the thread.

But no, first fresh tears as the phone rang and relief in sight, in reach. A mother had bought this skirt, one of dozens hanging there, to protect the fragile cloth that wrapped the leg bones and pads of fat and muscle. The skirt was a mother's armor. Sybele often accused Siri of treating her like a maid, but valet was more like it—varlet, as Shakespeare might say—one who armed the knight for battle. Siri picked up the receiver.

It was Sybele, and Siri cried into the phone like a newborn baby.

And here was Esther, mouth dropping open. Siri turned her back, but talk was impossible. Sybele screaming and weeping at the other end and those cold, inquiring eyes sweeping the room. "I gotta go," she told her mother and hung up.

The phone rang. "Hello," Esther said. "No, she's not

here. I know she was talking to you, but she's gone now. She went to the bathroom. Shall I—?" Esther looked at Siri, who was wiping her face with a tail of the bedspread. "She hung up on me," Esther said.

The phone rang. "Tell me what to say to her!" Esther said.

Siri considered. "Tell her I'll call her back."

"Hello? Listen—. Listen—! Mrs. Sorenson!" Esther hung up. "She's calling the state police."

"Call her back."

"What's her number?"

Siri called out the number, but the line was busy. "It's busy," Esther said. "She must be calling the cops."

Siri smiled just enough to show a sliver of teeth.

"She won't call the state police, will she?"

"She's calling my father."

"Oh, well. That's not so bad."

The phone rang. "Hello," said Esther. "Oh, hi. Yes, she's here." She handed the phone to Siri. "It's your father."

"Tell him I'll call him back."

"Can she call you back?" Esther listened. "He needs to talk to you. He won't hang up until he's heard your voice. Tell him you're okay," she whispered, "even if you're not."

Siri took the phone. "Hi, Dad." She listened. "No." She listened. "Yes." She listened. "Not anymore. I'm fine now." She listened. "Hi, Mom." She listened. "You must have heard wrong. No, I didn't say anything. Nothing happened, Mom. I had a bad dream." She listened. "I don't remember." She listened. "I'm okay now. Don't worry. Stop crying now." She listened. "I'm fine. Here, talk to Esther.

She'll tell you I'm fine."

Esther took the phone. "Yes." She listened. "I'm looking right at her. Yes, we had dinner together. Pancakes. Yeah, I know. Cottage cheese. She's fine, Mrs. Sorenson. She must have taken a nap. No, I've been here all afternoon. Everything's fine now." She listened. "Cross my heart and hope to die." She listened. "Goodbye, Mrs. Sorenson. Nice talking to you. No, she went out to get a drink of water. Yes, thank you. I'm fine. Yeah. Tomorrow she'll call. Yup. Bright and early. Bye now." She listened. "Hi, Mr. Sorenson. Yes. No, not tonight. Tomorrow. Will that be okay? Good night now."

Wondrously, when Esther hung up the phone and thought to pull its plug, Siri did feel better. The pain was fainter and, big deal, as Esther would say, the deed was done, the cookie crumbled. No one would know or care, unless she told them about it. It was a tree falling in the forest with no ears or eyes to see or hear.

It was an event, yes, and the aftereffects, the "telltale" signs, as an old-fashioned person would say, might be visible, but even Esther, studying as hard as she could, and with her glasses on, could only see—Siri jumped up to see in the mirror what Esther was seeing.

She was radiant. The tears had dried, the eyes clear. She was fatter, blown up and puffed out. The cheeks were rosy and the lips pink. Next to this icon—for a second head had appeared in the mirror—was Esther with rings under her eyes and tired, oily skin and hair like a Brillo pad and all that angst of daily failure at the keyboard, in the classroom and in the listening room, etched on her face.

"Look at me," Siri said, pointing to the head on the right.

"Look at *me*!" Esther said, nodding to the head on the left.

"So, what happened?" Esther asked, when they both had looked long enough.

"What do you mean?"

"Why are your parents so upset? What'd you tell them?"

"I didn't tell them."

"Didn't tell them what?"

Siri thought. Was the cat out of the bag already, or only half out? She looked at Esther's big, tired face. She loved Esther. Esther was a true friend. Esther had taught her to read and write. Siri smiled with this radiant, new face. She could feel the smile stretching through the tear-stiffened skin.

"Are you crazy?" Esther said. "Talk to me!"

"An awful thing happened, Esther, but I turned it into something good."

Esther sat on her bed.

"I had sex with Mr. Farrand, and I came to consciousness."

"What?"

"Just as I said. The physical act broke me out of my waking dream."

"I don't believe this. Why are you saying this?"

"It's true."

"If it's true you need to call a doctor. Call the police, too."

"Why?"

"Sex with a minor is a crime."

"It is?"

"Did Farrand do this to you?"

"Nothing happened. It wasn't that big a deal."

"Yes it was! I heard you crying on the phone. Now your family's all upset. It was a big deal, unless you're crazy and making the whole thing up."

Siri lay on her back with her hands folded over her waistband. She smoothed her skirt, but Esther had already noticed the wrinkles and scuff marks.

"Maybe you should take that off," she said. "Are you hurt?"

"Only a small part of my body. My back is a little scratched, too."

Esther helped Siri pull off the skirt. Esther saw some blood. "Let's throw this out," she said. "Okay? No cleaners will get those stains out. The lining's ripped, too. This whole thing," Esther said, "is making me very sad."

"Don't be sad, Esther," Siri said. "It's too late. I've already got what I want from it."

"It really happened?" Esther shrilled. "He did *this* to you?"

Siri looked at Esther's shocked face. There was meaning in it, but before responding to it, she had to parse the sentence just offered. She was puzzled by the word order. "He" was the subject, and "you" was the object of the preposition. "He" was first and "you" was last and connected to the sentence only by the loose link of a "to." "*This*" was in the middle, separated from "he" and "you" and rising a little above the rest because of its importance.

She tried it out like a glove over something shapeless.

"He" was okay: that was the thumb, but how were the four finger pouches supposed to fit? Where am *I* in this? In philosophy, the easiest operation was to reverse the terms and restate the proposition in a calm tone: "I did this to him."

Siri looked at Esther. Esther was shaking her head no. "That's a crazy thought." But the way she said it—quiet and dreamy—meant that, for the moment, Siri was absorbed by the experiment, by the loft of the trial balloon.

Who rightfully belonged at the top of the sentence? He, I—or, Siri looked at Esther with wide eyes. We? "*We* did this to me?"

Esther was ready to bite. "We did this to you," she repeated.

Siri laughed. "It's true, isn't it? We did this to me. I meant Dr. Farrand and me, but it's really you and me who did this to me."

"That's not a sentence that means much in English," Esther said, "if the sum of we and you is only two people. If it's three people—Dr. Farrand, me and you—that makes sense. It's a meaning sentence."

"Maybe 'we' isn't right. 'I' is not right and neither is 'he.' He's a jerk, Esther!" she said. "He's a complete jerk."

"You're the one who told me that," Esther said, "that day I came back from Wellesley."

"Esther," Siri said, "should it be: we did this to him?"

Esther laughed. "Maybe, but is he home crying right now, like I saw you?"

Siri flushed. She refused to attach this rich and strange flood of feeling to the agency of a complete jerk. She raised a hand to stop Esther from speaking.

"*This* is an important term in the proposition, Esther, and we haven't yet put it into question."

"That's the hard one, Siri. It's good we're leaving it for last. We need to work up to it." Esther was still holding the skirt by the waistband. "Can we talk about something practical for a minute?"

"I don't care. Go ahead. I'll remember where we left off. How could I forget?"

"Are you okay?"

"I guess so. Everyone goes through it, right, at one point or another?"

"True, and you've gotten it out of the way early."

"Do you think this is early?"

Esther considered. "Well, think of the girls on this floor. How many do you think have really done it? I don't care how many 'weekends' they've gone to. Most of them are holding out. What do they have to dangle over some jerk's head, but that? That's how they get the frat pin and then the engagement ring. Are you listening to me?"

"I'm counting. I can think of one or two I know that've done it."

"How do you know for sure?"

"I know what it is now."

Esther considered. "If you know, why don't you tell me?"

Siri looked. "You already know. Everybody knows in the abstract. They know the steps. They just don't know how it feels."

"How does it feel?"

"Not good, but I haven't decided. It depends, doesn't it,

on the outcome of the sentence? I could like it better, or I could like it worse."

"You mean it's something—even when it's done to you—you can't decide about?"

"Not finally. It's like any other experience in that way. It has to be weighed and interpreted. Otherwise, it's just pointless sensation."

"If you really mean that, you're over the line."

"What line?"

"Where the mystics went."

"Imagine," said Siri. "How did it happen?"

"Are you glad it happened?"

"I don't know. It's too early to tell."

"Is it terribly uncomfortable?"

"I'm getting used to it."

"Are you still bleeding?"

"What?"

"Put your bathrobe on and give me your clothes. Then, take a shower."

"You think I should?"

"You're a little too far out on a limb. Thinking needs physical props, Siri. Certain things have to be under control."

"They do?"

"I think so. I don't know. I never got as far as you. The body's just clay and it gives out after a while. Same thing happens to musicians. These high functions take their toll."

"How's music?" Siri asked, sitting up.

"Lousy," said Esther. "I'm lousy at it. Even I can tell, and my ear isn't that good. I have no talent for it."

"So why're you doing it?"

"I love it. It's fun just to be around it. The dumbest music major has something to teach me, even when they can't talk worth a damn."

"What about your teacher, Madame Bovary?"

"Madame Bovary doesn't talk. She just hits."

"She hits you!"

"Practically."

"Why?"

"She doesn't want to teach someone like me. I remind them all," Esther said, tears rolling down her cheeks, "of all the mistakes they've ever made, or what a dead end it is, even for them, even for Madame. Music outstripped them. It does for all but the very best. And the difference is as clear as a bell. No one is mistaken or deluded, not even the stupidest."

"Are you talking about yourself?"

"No."

"Are you talking about me?"

"No."

"You're making me feel very alone, Esther, even though you're here with me."

"We're both alone. That's why we get along."

"That's *not* why we get along."

"Maybe not."

"We get along because you've taught me everything I know until recently, when now I know more. And you wear my clothes and use my money to buy books. Or you used to, when you bought books."

"That's true. But we're also friends, aren't we?"

"I'm not sure I know what that is."

"You may not know, but you're living it."

"Together? Equally?"

"Yes. And for no good reason except this academy of fools threw us together."

"Oh, yeah," Siri said, smiling. "I remember the academy of fools."

"I thought you would."

"Am I there yet, Esther, there where you were trying to get me?"

"I can't even remember what I had in mind. Whatever it was, you've far exceeded it. You've overrun the mark. You said that yourself."

"Thanks."

"I'm glad," Esther said, "you still think it was a good thing."

"I didn't say that. I thanked you for giving me my start. The goodness of it is unclear. There are too many basics I still need to work out. The simplest sentence is a mystery to me."

" 'He did this to you'?"

"For example."

" 'A fool is amazed by every word'?"

"Amen."

"And we do know, don't we, what we mean by fool."

But Siri wanted to finish the dialogue on love as Plato had—alone—or just with Socrates, using the peripatetics as a foil. Esther had to practice. Even to be a dumbbell in music, you had to practice many hours, give your life over to it.

Thinking, on the other hand, was a life of infinite stretch. Thinking accommodated everything and everyone. It was free, it could be hidden, it needed nothing, but could use whatever was available. It had no needs or requirements.

Instead of using up a life, as music was using up Esther's, it gave a second life, a double thickness. Esther didn't have to spell out its value because Siri knew from experience. It was like having a private car in an old-fashioned train, always on the move, nosing into this and that. You sat on a comfortable seat behind the glass and life came to you, brushed past your face, just fast enough to see but not to stultify.

Siri closed her eyes. Esther covered her with a quilt and turned out the light. "Goodbye," she said, "for now."

So this was college, Siri thought, as a pair of thin lids dropped on swollen eyeballs. In the cranial space was a wonderful, living photograph—more like a holograph without the smoky light. There were Sybele and Dad on their date. He was hustling her into Kirkland House—and Siri knew what would follow.

Teddy was in his playpen, eating the crayons that Siri—who was invisible—had just given him, ones she didn't need: the white and the black, the brown, the gray and the flesh-colored. He tasted them all and was chewing on the paper. Bad! She was bad, Sybele was saying, grabbing the crayons from Teddy's moist fists and digging the chunks of black from his toothless mouth.

Turn the page. And here was Esther, or was it Irene? If

Siri wasn't careful, the cranial stage would crowd with people, one behind the other, like cards in a deck, arranged by suit. Christo and Esther and Dad and Teddy, Sybele and the nuns and Madame and Eiki Paik. Siri wasn't a card, but she held them all and played them on the tray in the moving train.

Was Dr. Farrand in there? Was Mr. Whitman? Dr. Farrand's card had slipped off the tray. You were always losing cards in this game, because they were thin and slippery. New cards were available, but a limited number, and up to the dealer to dole them out. Where was the dealer? Siri was grasping, or groping for his identity when the lights went out and the real dream began.